EXILE

Also by Robert Nichols

Slow Newsreel of Man Riding Train*
  (poetry, 1962)

Address to the Smaller Animals†
  (poetry, with Lucia Vernarelli, 1976)

Red Shift: An Introduction to Nghsi-Altai†
  (novel, with Peter Schumann, 1977)

Arrival: Book I of Daily Lives in Nghsi-Altai
  (novel, 1977)

Garh City: Book II of Daily Lives in Nghsi-Altai
  (novel, 1978)

The Harditts in Sawna: Book III of Daily Lives in Nghsi-Altai
  (novel, 1978)

*City Lights Books
†Penny Each Press

ROBERT NICHOLS

EXILE

BOOK IV OF
Daily Lives in Nghsi-Altai

A NEW DIRECTIONS BOOK

Exile is the fourth volume of the tetragology DAILY LIVES IN NGHSI-ALTAI. I *Arrival.* II *Garh City.* III *The Harditts in Sawna.* IV *Exile.* The first three books were published, respectively, in 1977, 1978, and 1979.

Portions of the "High Mass/Energy Canticles and Sacred Formulae" first appeared in *New Directions in Prose and Poetry 26.* "The History of Nghsi-Altai" was originally published, in a somewhat different form, in *New Directions in Prose and Poetry 33.*

A passage from *Village Life in Northern India,* by Oscar Lewis, with the assistance of Victor Barnouw (Copyright © 1958 by The Board of Trustees of the University of Illinois) appears on pp. 7-8. It is reprinted by permission of Random House, Inc., and Harold Ober Associates, Inc.

Lines from Allen Ginsberg's "Howl," in *Howl and Other Poems* (Copyright © 1956, 1959 by Allen Ginsberg) are reprinted on pp. 74 and 75 by permission of City Lights Books.

Manufactured in the United States of America
First published as New Directions Paperback 485 in 1979
Published simultaneously in Canada by George J. McLeod, Ltd., Toronto

Library of Congress Cataloging in Publication Data
Nichols, Robert, 1919-
  Exile.
  (A New Directions Book)
  (His Daily lives in Nghsi-Altai; book 4)
  I. Title.
PZ4.N623Dai   Bk. 4 [PS3527.I3237] 813'.5'4 79-15330
ISBN 0-8112-0732-3

New Directions Books are published for James Laughlin
by New Directions Publishing Corporation,
80 Eighth Avenue, New York 10011

To my grandparents, Rose and Lavenus Lalone,
immigrants from Three Rivers, Quebec Province,
and others unknown.

CONTENTS

EXILE

HIGH MASS / ENERGY CANTICLES AND SACRED FORMULAE

WEATHER PATTERNS

1

The geese fly over

Early September (the month of Asauj)   thru mid-November
(Katik)   The poles tip.   Transit of the Autumnal
Equinox setting into motion the dry monsoon season

The weight of air   the subsidence
A polar wind pinched out of the air pressure differential
                        streams from the Siberian uplands
atmosphere of the Earth/   dragged by celestial mechanics

And rays of light broken/   from the upper sky
                        reflected from the clouds
The rest penetrate through   to Earth
And are convected back   as heat

The radiation budget
The immense heat engine   The thermocouple
                        at work
reversal of sky currents over Asia/   whole oceans
of atmosphere moving another way
Winter/Summer oscillations

And the Sea of Air
The majestic sweep and swap
                        of the continental air masses
with a shift of a few isobars
        1030 to 1028 to 1020 to 15 to 10
the polar front   slides out of the mountain slopes off
                        Heliunkiang
ice on the Yellow River

1

the fishing fleet off the jetty at Haiphon
        trims its sails
I touch   you my brother/Wind

The hills as aerofoil   on the mountain above Nghsi-Altai
accelerate the current sluicing it into the propeller blades
                     of the windmills
set at an elevation of 35 meters   with a swept area of
              2500 sq. meters
the wind is picking up speed/   at a threshold of
3/m/sec   the rotors begin to turn
Energy yield at 12.4/m/sec max./according to the formula
       $k\ (Tv^3 - d)$
       Praise the Altgaier wind charger

Praise him   the Danish inventor
They said of him the farmers of that area
Askov Denmark 1887
     about Poul la Cour that he could
"transform the rain and wind into electricity and heat"

Venu harvests   the wind

2   The Operating Procedure

We watched the weather anvil
the cold layer settling in over the Great Plain
High up the alto-cumulus
bruised storm masses/   lightning flashes between
          tattered dark cloud   then sleet
outriders of the wind
        catch the geese wings
Over the brown fields   the march of the power lines to Garh

That day the team of twelve or so Windmen were on the slab.
Snow dusted our parkas. At the edge of the slab a rabbit hole

2

partly covered and a scattering of dry leaves. The grip of cold iron
under the gloved fingers. A bright clinking of the chain echoes on
the ribs of the hills.

And the endless political meetings
"Up all night the interminable discussions and countless cups of
    coffee"
Getting the line straight. The ache of leadership goes through my
    bones.

3

The blades spinning/   not icing up yet
and the directional servomechanism working quite
                 nicely thank you

Winter
It's a hard gig

But in a couple of months and I'll be out of all this
back home fucking my wife

The march of the power lines to Garh

An hour after sundown
       stamped up and down in our felt boots
As we pulled the straw cloaks over our shoulders

we heard the geese bark
          navigating by the moon

The Rose of Winds favors us

THE MEANING OF FESTIVALS

1

A ray of sun breaks thru the clouds & illuminates
a field   And I am surrounded by light as if coming
from the white birches   or the snow on the ground/
thru which stalks of goldenrod lift up

weeds & the flowering crowns of ferns
                    touched with radiance
It is the meaning of the festivals revealed
so long hidden...

the brown skeletons of the ferns   the flute sounds
her cheek smeared with turmeric paste shines
                                    yellow   yellow
As the dancer raises her eyes to me
                    the river of time stops

2

The swirling street   Animals
crowds of people in costumes, masks
the dream spirals with the drum beat   in the heat
the revelers are throwing colored powder at each other
                        By the bank of the sacred river
the throng bathes   wedged against itself

As in the old story: A shout
"The bulls have been stolen   the royal doors
to the cattle shed have been broken into." We must follow
the thieves thru the suburbs under the banner of
                        the "Right Communists"
thru the mists of time

Firecrackers explode   the marchers have broken into a run

4

in front of the governor's mansion in Calcutta. My eyes
swim. We're backed to the curb. A procession of lanterns
the crowd separates & a cart is pulled thru slowly decorated
with flowers the bride proceeded by a limousine

                         her veil is the mystery.
The bulls are loose on the street
The crush deepens. The radio blares out
that the municipal power plant has been sabotaged

3

This is the way DEIR is performed:
on the day before: fast
        wash away the chaff from the threshing floor
        sweep the shrine   Women leave the lights on
        and go to the rooftop with your pitchers
        and pour out water to the moon

On the morning of DEIR:
        by this time the fireplace has been replastered
        the house machinery has been oiled and the tools put away
        The children may go around in groups begging for toys
        The Ganji Figure (tantra) has been incised on the wall
                in fresh plaster

At 2 p.m. or an appropriate time:
        The Household gathers and the story of Ganji is told
                Ganji—the Speedy One
        Each time a part of the story is completed one of
                the family shouts
        and the storyteller drops in a bean
        When the pot is full of beans   the story is ended.

The complete mantra for Ganji-Devi:

```
devi   devi   devi   Ga
                          sa bu   thanoi
devi   devi   Ga
DEvi   devi   ga
OM sabu   thanoi   om   ga
WEE   HA
WEE   HA
OOO   ri   ai   GAI   bha
              WEE   HA
              WEE   HA
OOO   ri   ai   GAI   SABU   THANOI
GA   OO   OM SABU   SABU   THANOI   BA
              WEE   BA
              WEE   BA
DEvi   devi   ga
RAmi   devi   ga
RAmi   RAmi   Ba
DEvi   ba
```

"BE IN GOOD HEALTH!"
(or a better translation:
may there be good public health)

4

The meaning of the festivals is revealed
                    as the snow melts from the hill
bare patches   of the earth
the stiff heads of weeds still up   and flying
                          their pennants
leftovers of the year
                    the Festival
And the long line of cars going out bumper to bumper
        "City traffic   it's awful   but it'll ease soon
                          as we reach the pike"

Headlights of the cars sweep the nite
the children asleep in the back seat
                            in their best clothes
"Going to visit grandmother
                    for the Holidays"

Wheels
the whole country on the move
                worshiping the GOD

Sing it!
"a poem is no more than a pair of tight pants"
                Frank ("Francis") O'Hara
killed Fire Island Atlantic sands
                        June 1961
by jeep taxi
                    ebb tide of the breath
Death among the seashells

GODDESS MOTHER MATTA PROTECT US FROM
                        CHOLERA
            PROTECT US FROM SMALLPOX
            PROTECT US FROM POWER FAILURES
            PROTECT US FROM BACTERIA MUTATIONS
GODDESS MOTHER MATTA PROTECT US FROM
                        SNAKE BITE
            PROTECT US FROM TRAFFIC ACCIDENTS
    BLOOD ON THE HIGHWAY
    SIV-RATTRI OF THE MIRACULOUS MEDAL
            PROTECT US FROM THE WEATHER
PROTECT US SIV-RATTRI MOTHER OF SULPHUR

5

"On Amavas day the cattle are not yoked but decorated with
reddish paste made of red oxide and oil. Spots are daubed on

animals sides and faces, their horns painted red, green, or blue.
Peacock feathers may be attached to their heads, while their
necks are hung about with beads, necklaces, and leathery bands
clinking little bells."

The tools "worshiped" and put away
    & the "bitauras"
the concentrated energy-packets blessed
    high energy phosphate bonds

The flux of the year organizes itself
                            on the occasions of the Festivals
just as the stream of a man's life is organized
around the events of the age-grade societies
the growth stages

6   Mensas—A Calendar

PHAGUN (Feb. March)	SIV RATTRI	Weather changes Worship of the refrigerator
CAIT (May)	KRI KARALI	Ghi lamps are lit The child gets his first haircut
SAVAN (July)	TIJ	Swings hung from the trees Wrestling & menstruating exercises
ASAUJ (Oct.)	KANAGAT	Allhallows eve When the dead come back
POH (Nov. Dec.)	GOBARDAN MAKAR- SANKRANT	Regional Planning Festivities Quarrels are patched up Policemen's motorcycles are decorated
MAGH	BASANT	Grandfather Frost's day

8

(Feb.)   PANCHAMI   Last bags of rice are
                                         given away

"Tij comes and sows the seeds of the festivals
Holi takes them away and wraps the Festivals in her shawl"

and so the year passes

and so the year passes

7

In the heat of the courtyard   we are gathered this Amavas day

my brothers have swept the ground bare
                    in the newness of this holiday

& made the effigy on the wall
on the matrix of the bright whitewashed wall
                        on this fifth day

Pour buttermilk into Ganji's mouth
Our hands fashioning the picture out of cowdung:
                    MANKIND'S head and mouth

Sing the festival song:
                    on this the fifth day
          "GRANDMOTHER
COWDUNG WEALTH
          BE WITH US!"
                    from the neck the four walls of our house extended into
                        the landscape

contains us and the sacred animals
                              blessed be this Easter of the year
We fashion it out of straw
                        the model of the Celestial City

9

Weeds flame
       the head of goldenrod burns

FEAST MY BROTHERS

A DAY IN THE LIFE OF SATHAN

1

Now that my husband is crew chief   I am able to be at ease a little. I lie back in the hammock. On the roof with its blue tile is a lemon tree   and from the administration office below comes the clack-clack-clack of machines.

Bring me the report   I want to look at it. And bring me the computation sheets   I want to see the figures. The scene of the collective spreads out below. The shade of the glossy leaves of the lemons   falls on my arms.

"Raking up the Bitterness Sessions." The web of ties are like the locust branches in winter   their thorny spikes. How they cut the chest

My sons are going out. In a few hours you will hear the call of the men with the ox team. And the call of the cadre on the truck loading bay of the cannery. And my daughter Maddi will go out with her electrician's tools and repair the wires.

How blue the sky sparkles!

2

Husbands   am I attractive to you   Or do you find me plain in my padded coat? Is my hair hidden from you braided in a coil under my canvas cap? Can you judge how my legs move?

Husbands   do you find my daughter beautiful   with her
shawl woven of bright plaid   thrown over her shoulders?
Would you like to strip it off? Does her blouse please you
spangled with silver mirrors?

The wash house is full of people. Billows of steam rise under the
rafters. The woman bends over the pile of clothes beside the
bathers   her buttocks gleaming. The door opens   from the
cold. As the laborers take off their frosty parkas   a breath of
winter steals out. And my flesh tingles

My flesh   my nipples washed with grass. It is sunset. Bring the
child to me here   and bring the brass tray with bunches of
striped kami grass to cleanse the breasts and to sweeten them. I
squeeze the first milk onto the tray and throw down a wrist bangle

In honor of my first-born

3

A shrill blast. The loudspeaker is calling from the top of the command post. And the people with the hard faces are streaming
across the snow

In the sweaty meeting room   the bowl is passed around. It has
been broken and mended, and broken and mended again. Drink
the bitterness from it   women with eyes hard as slate.

That history is over   the bad days are past. But sisters we have
elected to remember it.

The chairperson begins: I remember the sky dark with dust
we thought it was a locust plague   The fence posts were buried
in sand. A field of corn sailed over the barn

Then the secretary remembers: there was no hay. We beat the
donkey but he was too weak to   get up.

11

The treasurer of the marketing section   we kept going down the road. Grandfather and Varya were pulling the cart. It had all our belongings in it   the sink and a crate of chickens. The army was like a river   we kept pushing against the stream of soldiers

Fill the bowl with the bitter herbs   drink from it, you have only remembered half of it

A woman says: that summer we were on the Delta. The ground dried up   it was baked. A corpse lay on it

And another says: then the flood waters went away. We came down out of the trees.

Another   says: That winter the city was without coal

No   I can't eat the elm leaves   they make my stomach sick. But the roots can be chewed

I would walk. Yes I would gladly sell the child for 5 annas. I would take her and carry her to the crossroads where the helicopter is hovering and the officials are giving out medicines. But my feet are bound

"Raking up the Bitterness Sessions." The fire is down. But if there is a coal of   hatred   among the ashes blow on it

4

The scene spreads out to view. Sometimes the road is lost between the narrow walls   a maze of alleys open from the bazaar. At the edge of town   it emerges again   a white stroke   baked onto the fields. The High Road

Through the region   the rivers run down, melting under the ice of Altai. There is a river running beside Watermeadow, where the

12

council meets. There is a river running through the Lake Sections,   through the forest cantonments where the universities
are located. There is a river running under the Rift Cities. And in
the dry Plains   it runs under the windmills

Clouds gather in the sky. And in the market place they have set up
a speakers platform. In the dust   in front of the platform
children are playing.

A woman has pushed forward from the crowd. She has lifted one
child up on her shoulders so the speakers can see him. Another
child held by the hand   presses close to her

And I ask the sky: Will you be luminous enough? Will you have
enough   warmth? And I ask the earth: Will you be full enough
     Earth will you have enough milk   to nourish this woman's
breasts?

Woman   with the hard face and rough hands I draw you aside
     I push the rough cloth from your breasts and kiss them.
     Sister   I embrace you

And your children   whose are they?

5

It is the Festival of Girdi-Divali   marking time of the new year.
It is necessary to distribute the new rice. The trucks of the Buyers'
Co-operative have arrived. We will distribute the radios.

I   raise my arms over the tiles washed by the blue sky. The
lemon tree is a storehouse   the flesh is full of oil   the skin
of the fruit glistens

Open the cupboard. It is enough if I say to you: the sun is drying
the clothes.

13

Now it is necesary to make an inventory. For instance there are beehives. In the garden a hummingbird is going back and forth over the petals. It is enough if I say to you: the sea is making salt

In the planning room of the commune   the officials have gathered. We have maps and production estimates. We have the models for the next year's development which the computer has organized.   Let us choose the options:

For instance
there is the nutrient budget. For instance there is a heat budget. There is an energy budget. For instance a man with his bare hands on a hectare of ground   will perform in a day 600 calories of work. And with an investment of capital in a machine he will perform 1800 calories.

There is the population budget. This is the array of facts   and these are the limits. It is necessary for us to calculate.

On the roof   I lie back on the hammock. The scene of the collective spreads out to view. The breeze lifts the leaves of the lemons and strokes my arms.

Sisters   in our hands

        the abundance.

THE COMING OF NEW MAN

1

Across the veld   the coming of New Man
The distances divide   A thorn tree is on fire against the azure
a glass jar at the base   tells us half the truth

Leaves plummet   It is *as if*

the world were burning up in autumn
a smoky haze   strips the hills bare / and evaporates

Oh   I am dazed with seeing / his house   down to the
    smallest detail
You too, traveler, will taste the salt on his skin
as the caravan appears   through the dust / cluttering the
    horizon

Across the dunes & shuttling oases the great distances over the
    desert —
Tashkent Sinkiang Lop Nor   Ama Attu —
are covered by the light leap of a gazelle
                  my song to you
                 Venu: New Man

2

Woman of a 1000 years hence   I don't know you
Man of a 1000 years hence   I don't recognize you

And the cities of the airy dawn

     Solieri's City of Light/   & concrete nodes
                         spun out like vertebrae

     Kikutate's Perforated Cylinders/   sunk under the sea
        with their great shopping centers & apartments
           powered by algae and phosphorus

     Isamov's Modulors with their etherealized machines
        suspended between Spitzbergen & mainland Russia

Chicago of the double helix
                  lifts   on the next tide

Tear down the walls. It's imprisoning us this pyramid
                                 this ziggurat
heaps   of scrap   & tangled conduit   the Eagle/   the
      Fasces

We will need dynamite   bulldozers to clear a path
The obstruction is in our midst
                  a thin door of steel/
                              seals the backs of our eyes

3

Bride   GO to meet the bridegroom
It is the Time   of trembling & fear   but GO OUT
to meet him   holding your lamp high
         against your face
When he touches you   you will be changed
                                 beyond recognition

Blind one   your eyes   Oh the pain of opening them
      how difficult it is for you
Reluctant one   your flushed skin

Bride   go to meet the bridegroom/   When we touch
I see I have repelled you
                  the flesh turns away

4

The leaves plummet   an autumn fire
strips the hills bare
Visions of the New World   of Albion
After the War decades   the smoke lifts
over the valley of broken wagons

by the river bank   the curve of houses
it is the same roofs   the same TOWN
                that we always knew
     – but hidden   from   us

Oh   cityscape   how I have longed for you
The bolts at the back of eyes   drawn
     the freshness of prima verde
Fra Angelica's colors
     the blue   the umber   the yellow cinquefoil
Going   back to him   thru the fields
     this spring day!

5

By the thorn tree we came upon his camp
But he'd gone   leaving noting but a direction signal
                        & a broken bottle

The immense distances over the veld
over the horizons   of time
                Is there some formula we can use
a sine curve or projection showing
how the electrons stream out of the rocks shown by an
     absorption spectra?
            the genetic drift

Scratchings on the cave wall in Lascaux
and I the artist
                draw tomorrow's Sun
                & the game we have to catch
the hunter draws on the wall in red oxide
            it is the ikon /
                New Man: the quarry
the solar wind

Mother   of   Animals
from your navel   a cord winds across the picture
            to the arrow
                    my canticle to you
                        New Man

In the sky with its jets/   the vapor stream condenses
                    my song to you/
                        New Man

6

Night evaporates   On the hill   the first spark
The light strikes New Man's porch
        the prophecy
                    and falls on a chair   a table
Window of this poem   I want you to frame
                    every utensil that he uses
The day   flames
he raises porridge to his lips

AMULETS OF THE BLUE SHAMANS

The sign   on the forehead: the hexagon
        (a double circle intersected by triangles)

Color: .35 – 45 microns (between blue and ultraviolet)

Sound: speech

Ornaments/decorations:
                on the wrist an ear of corn/   welded
                about the neck   feathers
                    middle technology totems
                about the ankles   poplar leaves   twisting
                        little propellers

18

Meaning of the hexagon:
    The Spaces

           THE CITY
           THE PLAINS
           WILDERNESS

           FREE MARKET
           THE PLANNED
           THE HOLY

The corresponding images

           FIRE
           TOPSOIL
           WATER

           THE CURRENT
           THE RULER/THE FULL MOON
           SUN/SKY

The tribes or tendencies

           THE STEELERS
           TRACTOR OPERATORS
           SLIDING FISH OR RAIN PEOPLE

           FILTHEATERS
           SOREHEADS
           STUNNED/BY/BRIGHTNESS PEOPLE

Formula: $E = hv$ (h = Planck's constant)

Degree or mode
of operation: photo-chemistry   or/alternately the
                Fibonacci series

The Blue Shamans   move with the wind
                         uphill
   and release the thistle

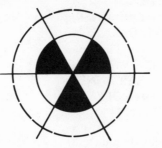

BLUE SHAMAN'S EMBLEM

AMULETS OF THE YELLOW SHAMANS

The sign on the forehead: two superimposed triangles

        black   to black   to black
              the outer dark
                  streaked with fire
            where the earth has cracked open

Direction: downward & inward

Mode: force/cataclysm

        the boat of the Yellow Shamans
                  navigates the cataract
          by banging against the rocks

Their dress:
        Frayed sleeves   yellow robes
          Priests/
              of the rotting grain sacks

        The line   grows thinner and thinner
             beyond my Fifth Ancestor

till it breaks into mist
(his breath on the window?)

Ornaments/decorations/masks:
      a man's forehead and behind
         a little furnace or box
            where the magnet revolves

Sound: replication/
      the printing press

To the fringes of the garments of the Yellow Shamans
      everything is attached
           thongs
           strings
           radiation particles
           threads
           bits of atomic debris
           wire
           keys
           strands of dirty raffia
           newsprint

Formula: $E = mc^2$

Their world   an explosion between
            the teeth

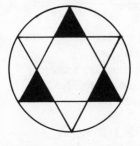

YELLOW SHAMAN'S EMBLEM

SAINT FRANCIS' CANTICLE

(Translated from the Italian by William Blake)

Most high encompassing good lord god
Breath of Being
Hear our praises   they belong to you
along with the glories and the sacred songs
They are all thine   Shining One

Praise be to you   and to ALL CREATURES
especially to my worshipful Brother SUN
thru whom you bring heat and brightness
He is beautiful and radiant with a very great splendor
Our Source
but he is only a pale signal from you

Praise to God for our most graceful Sister   MOON   and for
     all stars
and galaxies by the millions
The heaven is full of them   lost in space. In the darkness
you have found them. The intensity amplified.

Praise be Javeh   for our blustering Brother   WIND
This region's clan emblem
and for air and clouds and all weather
for our counsin the Wet Monsoon out of the east
and the Dry Monsoon out of the west
Windy lineage brother

Praise be my lord for our radiant Sister   WATER
who is pure and transparent
and very precious in the dry season
and lies at the bottom of the quanats
who is raised thru the pipes

Praise be to thee for Holi Region
which we perceive with our five senses extended by X-rays

22

All praises be for all
  earth/air cosmos infinite membrane
and for the wave of process from which ocean escapes

While walking in paradise I saw Altai
      which is common
also its mirror image Albion — now called
     America — which is extraordinary

God of the Double Shamans
  in your energy you have created them both
From the rags of your coat
  hang an infinity of worlds

Praise be to thee for Francis' festivals
  who named the days of the world
and who walked out of the devil's city in yellow and blue
  Umbria
   as out of a cave
and stripped off his clothes
     for Giotto to paint him in future flesh

SAINT FRANCIS' CANTICLE

(Adapted by William Morris)

O wide wordless limitless sweet lord God
we praise thee Nameless One
our rites science and our sacred songs
emanate from thee Shining One

We praise thee for the radiant and splendid Sun
power source
for moons/stars without number
and for all galaxies flung in space

We praise thee for our own language

and for the mysterious grammar of relationships
the miraculous metaphor
by which we pray to thee: "Father"·
and reach out to the earth: "Mother"

We praise thee for the mantle and Topsoil of the earth
which is gentle and mellow and serviceable
and can be ploughed
for Fire and all metals and elements
and for the oxygen that moves our lungs

We praise thee for the lovely molecule Water
transparent and changeable
a light airy vapor which condenses into a lake
cool under the sands of Altai
We praise thee for Wind   our brother

Praise be to thee Lord for all tools and technologies
for that special artifact of our hands
                              City
and for the Countryside half made
                        where we go in and out
and for Wilderness   unmade

We praise thee for all species/varieties/contradictions
which together make up Open Steady State
     which is our state   stateless
In Francis' name I walked into Trafalgar and Haymarket
to protest the war   And looking for Other World
          in their eyes   and my eyes

The rattle of machine guns.

SONG

Civilization thieves the flowers
and weaves them into Elizabeth's coronal
I will be the singer mild
who unravels those ceremonies
and returns stolen properties

But how can I give them back to old hands
                  ploughed   underground?
the Chams watched the locomotive smoke cut thru the vines
Malraux saw them and he told me so
in a book made of bones

So I won't go after Queen Elizabeth's coronal
but with Blake love the chimney sweeps
I will will them my forgeries
and for their sake invent fantastic technologies

SACRED FORMULAE FOR EARTH/SPACE SHIP

The rose of winds   favors us
if we are not already   annihilated
we will die into it   the windstream on my face
tide of cold air off Heliankiung
                  tips the propeller blades
Power floodgate opens   my mouth in praise
      for Earth/Space ship
red rose petal set spinning in space
            Every direction of the current tosses our boat
the terrestrial magnet   Out   to all points
                  vacancies   force fields
streams of lumens in between   space
our necks cricked to look up
            no other way   the taste in the mouth

25

my cheek red   registers the cold
                                    isobars
fall of sky pressure   on earth
My eye reading the instrument gauge is Thine

Chrome cups of the anemometer spin at night   prayer wheel
anchored in basalt rock   iron earth core
also the geotherm gives up its steam   prayer
                    Sun's radiance caught on the roof
where the children are singing their morning school
                                    biology anthem
sacred/

        the array of mirrors reflected onto the steam boiler
                Maddi is taking a public bath
her skin   red rose   earth petal   sky atmospheres
                                    condensed
flowers around the milkhouse
the cows browse and allow us to steal milk
                        for solar processing

Pasteur's lovely spirit presides
the saint in the ikon   212 degree holiness
Yes thank you Pasteur is alive and well for the future
in his white coat   boiling off microbes

Earth/air science   wind/rose   space   ship
                    infinite accumulations
        as the leaves fall
they yield in a million years   3 or 4 inches topsoil
our precious knowledge and store
        we're stored there   in earth/space cupboard
I saw in a museum near Uppsala
                        the boat dug out of the bog

wood black and hard as coal
      the stem and ribs remain
a few gold bracelets and eye   sockets of the wayfarers
            lost in soil
          moving thru earth/time
we stumble thru the corn   shucks
this song on our lips   for   the new commune

Every direction of the current orders our boat
from the terrestrial magnet   out
                    to all points
of the wind/rose   star/space miraculous commune journey
      the sun's rays gathered into our hands
as the old food-gatherers brought back wild rice in their canoes
      baskets of seeds/energies
      fantastic blackberry furnaces burn on each bush
         hand   steel   computerized instruments
                bloom
sacred technology smoke   around the temple swallowed in
  palms
each day the Chams watched the locomotive smoke out cut
  thru the woods
              carrying International Harvester tools
the topsoil
           so easy to break   easy to renew
compañeros   the Rome Plow broken at last

Brothers I come to prophesy
Open the doors of the boxcar and let me out
you standing along the forlorn rails
     the hammers on yr shoulders
        in the Polands with the blue railway stations
I come to bring you the good news
      State's withered
    old sticks/rags/ magics transmuted

Bakunin in his fat anarchist pajamas   old foolishness
                         but the wand flowers

heat latent in the song   bangs the pipes
          Oh sweet weather hammer
                         sleet   slants
and every drop of rain fires the forge

THE HISTORY OF NGHSI-ALTAI

We have been given the following brief history of the country of Nghsi-Altai. It seems curiously like our own — with some features reversed, as if seen in a mirror. It is impossible to fix any correspondence in dates. Presumably "present time" refers to something like our own present, extended forward somewhat. It should also be noted that our informant has given a biased account, being one of the Blue fraternity.

Prehistory: Forest covered the world, according to old legend. It was the era of the so-called "Walking Trees." For a long time the trees with their dense tops were able to keep out Sky, so the story goes. One day the trees weakened. Sky punched a hole in and entered accompanied by her brother, a monkey called Weather.

The southern half of the world was flooded and drowned in lakes. The north half received no water at all; it became dry steppe. The sun turned all the steppe-dwellers (men, ostriches, goats, and camels) as brown as dung. The rain falling in twilight turned the skin of the forest dwellers blue as lichen.

A wall was built between the West and the Dry by Monkey, which he called "The Divider." All elements of the world were separated: the Sky, Earth, and Forest, the west sacred men and the dry men. They conspired to punish Monkey. The wall was thrown down into a ditch, the present Rift Valley, and the Karsts (Monkey's descendants) were given no skin color at all: they are albinos.

From the "three skins" and the "three weathers" (or types of environment) the fields of knowledge are supposed to have been elaborated: agriculture, the ecological sciences, and trade.

FROM THE FIRST THROUGH FOURTH MILLENIUM/ A PLAINS TRIBAL CULTURE

This period begins with neolithic village culture already established.

Grave diggings deep under the loessal soil show that there were three tribes living in the plains simultaneously. Archaeologists call these the "gray pottery" people—Yang Shao. The "black pottery" people—Lung Shan. And the "painted pottery" people: the Jats.

The Jats appear to have migrated from northern India via the Khyber Pass through Turkestan and Iran, where they learned bronze age techniques: metal-smithing, the wheel (for chariots), and writing. From the plateau they migrated eastward, a ferocious cavalry, across the desert, hopping from one oasis to the next and intermarrying with the local folk.

However, they finally reached the plains in a state of exhaustion, not as conquerors but as a conquered people. They were absorbed in part by the other two tribes, and the bronze age discoveries appear to have been suppressed during the first millenium. (Bronze war axes have been found in the graves buried *below* neolithic pottery.)

This is the period of village high culture (neolithic). From a number of epicenters the population spread through the plains. The pattern of movement operated in this way:

First there was the "mother village": a hundred or so pit dwellings surrounding a longhouse. This was attached to a cemetery presided over by the shaman (ancestor worship). All the great neolithic discoveries are in evidence here: house-building (posts with wattle-and-daub construction), pottery molds and kilns, spindle whorls and needles, stone polishers, the tools of agriculture, and the bones of domesticated animals: the dog, the sheep, pigs, horses, and cattle. There were also extensive cattle herds and the beginnings of rice agriculture.

This improved food supply increased the number of inhabitants in the "mother village." Several "daughter villages" would be established still using the same cemetery and under the authority of the original priesthood. In this way the plains were populated.

High village culture seems to have prevailed during the first three millenia—the settlements in much the same form as they are today. However, at the end of the third millenium there was a decline.

Bad agricultural practices. Overgrazing by cattle, the ploughing of unsuitable land for crops, and a prolonged drought brought an end to this early period. Much of the plains became dust bowl. Productivity declined in the pasture lands. The burning of cow dung for fuel removed it from re-use on the fields as fertilizer. On the little arable land that remained, the crop rotation system was abandoned.

Destruction of the irrigation system by rabbits.

Starvation threatened, with a rising population now divided into rich and poor. Under pressure of population the regular food chain was broken. It was no longer plant (grains and legumes) ——⟶ to animal (protein) ——⟶ to man, the original sequence. But simplified to the direct chain: Plant—⟶ to human. The property owners ate only black millet. While the tenants and a landless proletariat subsisted on rice gruel and during famine grubbed for roots.

This was also a period of the grossest sexual exploitation, the males becoming the chattels of the matriarchs.

Fortunately, this period ended with the discovery by Jats of fossil fuel. A fragment of "painted pottery" of the fourth millenium depicts what seems to have been a natural gas strike. With the development of this substitute fuel (that is, substitute for cow dung), it was possible to reverse the above cycle and restore productivity. the Jats also developed a primitive textile industry using synthetic fibres.

Thus they gained an advantage over the other plains tribes. Gradual extension of Jat hegemony in the latter half of the fourth millenium. Main features of the present-day culture are established; that is, the matriarchy, limited polygyny, and village exogamous marriage, conservative economic planning performed by the guilds, and government under the panchayat system.

Present calendar of holidays is set. Inauguration of the Great Festivals.

FOURTH THROUGH FIFTH MILLENIUM/ A KARST COMMERCIAL EMPIRE

It is thought that the Karsts were originally lake dwellers. With geological transformation of the plateau, dessication due to weather changes, and the gradual subsidence of the great Rift Valley, the area became the present Drybeds. The tribe continued to live there, inhabiting the beaks and dolomitic caves. From cave dwellers they became miners, excavating the subsurface for minerals. This was the source of their wealth.

The Karsts are a naturally egalitarian people, with a strong aptitude for mechanics. A corporation of free citizens developed the mines. Special machinery was adopted for digging, and for ventilating and pumping water. Through pumps the properties of air (also a vacuum) were discovered. This led rapidly to the discovery of other gases, and laid the foundation for their future chemical industry.

Thus hydraulics led to science, science to trade, and trade to the evolution of money and a competitive market system. Domination of the other territories followed. The earlier portion of the fifth millenium was the great trading period of the Karsts, with their merchants spreading over the plains and Drunes regions. The great city-based merchant houses joined with the local overlords in a profitable alliance. Usually one of the members of a Jat family was assigned to handle the Karsts' commercial affairs. These enterprising young men often became tax collectors.

The Rift Canyon was now completely urbanized. As trade developed there was further rationalization of industry, particularly metals and chemicals. With the spread of the industrial corporation and further capital accumulation, finally the entire Rift had been organized into a national industrial system centered upon the steel industry. The government was one of nominal parliamentary democracy, with two parties. One of these, the Managers, were in firm control. Opposed to them was a weak Decentralist Party.

Certain tendencies, however, favored the Decentralists. One of these was the rigidity of the economic system itself. Its very success hampered it. Inventions were held off the market by the monopolists. There was little adaptation of machines to changing circumstances, due to heavy capitalization and vested marketing arrangements. Ingenuity flagged. In pursuit of profit they abandoned productivity and even the laws of capitalist dynamics. In its partnership with business the state subsidized an inflated "public sector" which absorbed unemployables and bankrupt industries. However, this resulted in increased inefficiency and inflation. A large advertising and transportation sector, once a stimulus, now became a drag on the economy. Agriculture was depressed.

Opposed to all this, the Decentralists stood for flexibility and free application of current inventions, and also for the freeing of the satellite "countryside" from the metropolis.

At this juncture, there appeared on the scene two inventions of special consequence: one was the small and compact hydrogen furnace, to substitute for the huge blast furnace of the classical steel industry, and along with it the small planetary mill. At the same time, certain new processes (called "pugging") made it economical to work outlying low-grade ore deposits in the plains. This was done by certain native capitalists (Jats)—who became convinced Decentralists. Advances in computerization and micro-circuitry also favored small units. Thus, it became possible to have a regionally based, rather than national, metals industry. All these methods were outlawed by the Managers.

A state of siege was declared.

A black market developed, in which there was extensive bootlegging of the new techniques. Outlaw capitalist groups in the plains were soon to organize the machinery banks. They were allied in an underground network with urban squatters' groups and with workers of certain Karst industries who were beginning to call themselves "syndicalists" or "anarcho-syndicalists."

A split developed among the Decentralists—a part of whom became the "Decembrists." Relying on armed force and financing themselves by kidnapping and extortion, this faction went underground to develop "subregions." Their slogans were "Every village its own steel mill" and "Factories in the caves." However, the movement was so deeply infiltrated as to be rendered ineffectual. The other side pushed for a parliamentary solution. A revived Decentralist party won the next parliamentary contest and swept the elections.

33

They had not reckoned on the perfidy of the Managers. A counterrevolutionary coup soon followed. All the Decentralist officials (representing a majority of the people) were either killed or exiled.

The Mangers were more firmly in control than ever. By now they had adopted many of the technical innovations promoted by the Decentralists and absorbed the best ideas of the opposition. Thus, under the slogan: "Abolish the state," the state was able to perpetuate itself for a thousand years.

At the end of the fourth millenium there was a civil war in which the state fell and was replaced by authentic popular institutions. These are the urban factory "syndicates" and the farm collectives (run jointly with the machine banks) that survive to this day.

Golden Age of the Popular Decentralists.

SIXTH MILLENIUM TO THE PRESENT/
THE EXPLOSION OF A THEOCRACY

The original Thays and Deodars lived in the forest undisturbed. The Thays are a slight, fair-skinned people probably of Indonesian origin. The stately and blue-skinned Deodars are of Tibetan stock, deeply mystical practitioners of a nature animism. From the beginning the two peoples lived together amicably in the forest under a confederacy of tribes or "gentes." They were hunters and herb gatherers. The Deodars, in particular, were skilled in medicine. An early woodland Deodar, Orpheo, is supposed to have invented music, while listening to the sighing of boughs.

At the dawn of historical time the confederacy had no center, merely shifted in the woods. Its members practiced "swidden agriculture," that is slash and burn: planting their seeds in a clearing made by stone axes, then moving on. Their shelters were of bamboo and leaves caked with mud—pitched in places selected by the shamans.

With the penetration of the Drune by the Karsts in the middle of the third millenium, the confederacy dissolved. There was intense trade exploitation. The forest sellers widened their clearings to trade tea, tung oil, and indigo, also skins and the feathers of birds, in exchange of trinkets from the Karsts, and metals. They also took up basket-weaving for cash.

As there was a limit to the size of clearings but not to the rising productivity of the Karsts, whose manufactured products increased each year, the foresters ran into debt. They were also divided among themselves. The basket-makers became enriched. Gradually the consumption of luxury goods from the Rift gave rise to a privileged class of traders, landowners, and moneylenders.

This led to more intense exploitation of the Drune. Ponds were drained and the forest cleared to underwrite the establishment of native manufactures, including a large plywood industry using the complaisant Thays as captive labor. The Thay tribes became completely colonized by the Karsts, and today speak only the Karst language.

The Deodars retreated further into the woods. It was now necessary for them to survive in a world that had diminished to the smallest compass. They first lived in holes. From a sack slung over their backs they planted seedlings to restore their natural protective cover. Hunting in the shade, they survived on a diet of snails and the smallest birds. Their appetites dwindled.

Meanwhile their shamans had become smiths. They set up forges in the deep woods, operated by skin bellows decorated with feathers. There they worked the metal stolen or traded from the Karsts. They learned to draw wire: copper, for which there was only an ornamental use at the time, for jewelry. And steel wire, which replaced catgut for musical instrument strings.

It was at this time that the famous Deodar teaching institutions began. These had originally been "hospices," or hospitals. Diseases had infected the Drune from the Rift, among the most serious being syphilis. For some reason the highest incidence of this was among the former shamans. The disease was cured by herbal medicines. It has been said the practice of celibacy among the Drune priesthood originated at this time.

What had been at first hospitals over the course of time evolved into universities. As their herbal cures became known they attracted the sick; and their musical and decorative arts, preserved from an earlier age, brought wanderers and collectors of folklore from the more developed portions of the country. There were also serious students.

There is some irony in this. It is possible that the students, many of whom came from the ranks of the richest colonizers, were attracted on spurious grounds. Certain aspects of the teaching — those which seemed to give the most weight — were in fact incidental. One of these was the color of the instructors' skins. Originally blue had been considered a mark of laziness and inferiority by the Karst industrialists. Now it began to be thought beautiful, even mystifying.

Their Deodar practice of celibacy gave them a reputation for holiness which was little deserved. The priesthood was intensely secular. Animals were still their sexual partners. And they depended for maintenance of the population level on recruits from other parts of the country, whom though they instructed they often abused.

In any case the Blue Doctrine expanded.

It was natural that the first studies were of forestry, natural history, and public medicine — which were to become later the nucleus of the ecological sciences. Cultivators of the small and the complex, the sciences of the Deodars developed in the direction of microbiology. The first environmental testing devices were originated in the Drunes. Using their medical knowledge and their resonating wires, instruments of all kinds were elaborated, which gave precise ratios and measured the most minute differences among natural phenomena. There were also advanced studies of insects.

When communication was later reopened with the rest of the country, knowledge of these Deodar sciences spread throughout the plains and Drybeds. This period saw also the hiring of the first Sensors — to man testing laboratories associated with the early machinery banks and factory syndicates.

Towards the end of the sixth millenium there was renewed trouble in the Rift. The Decentralist technology had been consolidated after the Civil War and the anarchosyndicalist political system was relatively humane. But the economy was overproductive. Intensive development led to depletion of the natural resources of the country. Waste recycling was merely token; and schemes for the conservation of energy, through the exploitation of alternate resources, were abused by the bureaucracy.

The riches of the soil and subsoil were squandered in an orgy of materialistic consumption. Monoagriculture was ravaged by bugs, despite inspection stations at every border. Lakes and reservoirs were poisoned by manufacturers of chemicals who were, with characteristic hypocrisy, members of decentralized regulatory commissions. Atmospheric pollution increased. This was due primarily to the Jat gas engine which—though scrapped centuries before—had left poisonous residues and in some cases even affected the genes. With wasting of resources came unemployment, and with unemployment, poverty. There was general social unrest and violence; and the regional governments, which had originally been libertarian, grew increasingly harsh and repressive. Persecutions of students and intellectuals followed, and these fled to the Drune.

It is not surprising that the next period, which has lasted about four hundred years from the end of the sixth millenium, has been the most fruitful in Deodar history. It has been marked by two main developments: an intensive effort to extend theoretical ecology to regulate actual economic production throughout the country. And a radical transformation of the Deodar priesthood.

This latter point requires explanation. During the previous millenium the priesthood had been by philosophy and belief, quietist; by character retiring, and by diet somewhat debilitated. But it was revived by the persecutions. At the onset of the environmental crisis in the plains and Drybeds, political dissenters were granted asylum by the Deodars. With the worsening of the crisis, the regional police—organized into companies of "berserks"—actually pursued the dissenters into the Drune, and in the end the Drune was invaded and occupied completely. The Deodar priesthood committed by religion to nonviolence could now not help but put that doctrine into practice. Total nonresistance to force, at the same time total noncooperation was followed. Orders given by the conquerors were received but never carried out, and the invading bands were at first neutralized and later completely absorbed — not without a number of martyrdoms on the part of Deodar high officials. The theocracy was decimated — and transformed.

The country was now divided into two worlds. In both the environment was equally threatened. This challenge was tackled directly — principally by the scientist-exiles (from the plains and Rift) now associated with the Drune universities. A new conservation and resource technology came into being, directed toward maintaining population and resources in dynamic balance in what came to be called the "open steady state planning." For this a new "embryology computer" became a chief instrument.

A key element in all this were the microtechnologies and sciences. Developed centuries before the Blue priests, purely to celebrate their own mysteries and out of a sense of the playful, these aptitudes of the Deodars became suddenly useful. And their practicioners, who had by temperament and historical development been at the margin of history—now moved to its center, as everything else failed.

The Deodar priesthood came to govern the country by accident, and as it were in spite of themselves, with the breakdown of all other institutions.

Religion revived based on the "Six Tendencies," which had survived from the ancient animism. The cult radiated outward, borne both by the squatters who had repopulated the devastated cities and by the Sensors who migrated in ever-increasing numbers back into the Rift and plains. As the authority of the Managers declined, that of the young Sensors attached to the Weather and Soils stations was strengthened. With the worsening of the ecological crisis the Sensor stations tended to take over certain functions of the local administration, until finally the state was absorbed completely.

Thus what came to be called the "Blue Revolution" and the "Magical Hexagon-in-balance" radiated outward from its many centers.

At this juncture a decisive and quite fortuitous event tipped the balance: the discovery of electricity in one of the forest universities by a Drune named Mazdo. This discovery was quickly applied, and grafted onto the traditional solar and wind technology, bringing universal benefits and enhancing immeasurably the authority of the new class.

Thus, under its double slogan: "Electrification/Conservation" and "A Blue World," the microscientific revolution was achieved, and the confederacy of Nghsi-Altai established in its present outline.

THE EMBRIOLOGY COMPUTER

The confederacy of Nghsi-Altai is an open steady state. An open steady state in nature maintains itself over varying periods of time. There is the water cycle, the carbon cycle. There is the geo-chemical cycle: the formation and weathering of rocks, the movement of the earth's crust, the laying down of ocean floors, the return through volcanoes of deep-core elements to the atmosphere. We say a "balance is kept" over a million years. Meaning: there is a grand swing and return. A cycle.

But in human society the dynamic balance—a state which is open and can take in new elements, yet is constant and self-sustaining—must be maintained by design. That is, by planning.

• •

We are designing a machine. (Actually the machine is in use in Altai. But we must reinvent it.) The first requirement: to calculate numbers and organize data on the model of an electronic computer. Also it must parallel living organisms, in that it must be capable of development.

Mechanical Requirements (simple computer model): typical nonlinear electric circuits in juxtaposition, with resistances, capacitors, inductances. Relays will be an electromechanical system with two alternative positions of equilibrium. The main synthetic functions will be: ARITHMETIC & LOGIC OPERATIONS, MEMORY (information storage), PROGRAMMING & FEEDBACK.

Diagram of typical relay and circuit:

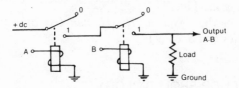

WEINER ON THE HUMAN BRAIN

This perceptive man (incidentally a real anarchist) makes a comparison between the human brain and a calculating machine. Both use the binary system. "The data are presented by a set of choices among a number of contingencies and the accuracy is determined by the sharpness with which the contingencies are distinguished, the number of contingencies presented at every choice, and the number of choices given." Rules for combining this data follow Boolean algebra: that is, a Yes-No system of notation.

Elements of the computer are like neurons. The nerve cell may be taken to be a relay with the message fed in from free endings or sensory organs, through points of contact, the synapses. These synapses are either at rest or they "fire" when the action threshold is reached.

The memory is similar in both structures. The firing of the synapses may be "clocked"; that is, the impulses retained and held up until some future time. Thus memory is a loop. The manner in which the loop is closed determines how long and how deeply the information is stored, storage taking place either by the opening of new paths or the closure of old ones. Apparently, in biological development no new neurons are formed in the brain after birth.

Weiner quotes from Balzac's novel *La Peau de Chagrin* and speculates that perhaps our whole life is on this pattern and "the very process of learning and remembering exhausts our power of learning and remembering until life itself squanders our capital stock of power to live."

Finally, there is the matter of self-regulation. The brain and the computer both regulate themselves. This is done by a feedback device which in biology is called "Effective Tone."

Our computer has its conditioned reflex. It has become in effect a "learning machine."

(From Norbert Weiner, *The Human Use of Human Beings: Cybernetics and Society.*)

A METAPHOR FROM BIOLOGY

How are we to enter upon the terrain of biological science? The first rule is not to consider this realm conceptually closed. Though it contains, it is like a torn fishnet. One must look at the grid for what it contains and for what it does not contain.

Thus we regard the biological sciences not as a map to follow with all its roads and connections, but as a field to pick flowers. Here "flowers" are images.

TIME SCALES

"Not only must we study the hour-to-hour or minute-to-minute operations of living things as going concerns (the chemistry), but we cannot leave out of account the slower processes in the period ...of a lifetime, by which the egg develops into the grown-up adult and finally towards senescence and death. On a longer time scale there are phenomena which must be measured in terms of a small number of lifetimes; they are the processes of heredity by which characteristics of organisms are passed from parent to off-spring. Finally on a time scale of many hundreds of generations there are the slow processes of evolution." (From C. H. Waddington: *Nature and Life*)

We use the passage as metaphor. It provides us with an image: Time which like a wave of the sea or current of air extends the range.

THE CREODES

An organism begins life with certain hereditary materials which define how it will develop. These paths of development are stable; i.e., the direction in which the cell develops is, in Waddington's term, "canalized." It is inflexible in the sense that it has a tendency to reach the normal end result in spite of abnormal conditions. But it also has a measure of flexibility and a tendency to be modified in response to circumstances.

The organism develops through steps, phases of the biological continuum. At certain points, pathways branch off, and the individual can go either way. Embrionic development though "canalized" is a sequence of moving through these branching

43

paths (creodes). Through feedback there is a balance between this inflexibility and this flexibility.

The growing organism pursues its "developmental fate." The fate is not just its materials, its building blocks. It is a set of potentialities depending on the larger relationships. There is an architecture. As Waddington says, "The architecture of the body can be defined as a probability function spread through the whole of its space."

So the body politic has its architecture. It too has its probability functions, determined by planning.

AN EMBRIOLOGY COMPUTER FOR COMMUNITY PLANNING

Requirements:

I Must exploit all above elements of computer/human brain model.

II Must accommodate growth in the biological model (also solving the dilemma of control vs. flexibility).

III Must be non-technological; i.e. politically useful.

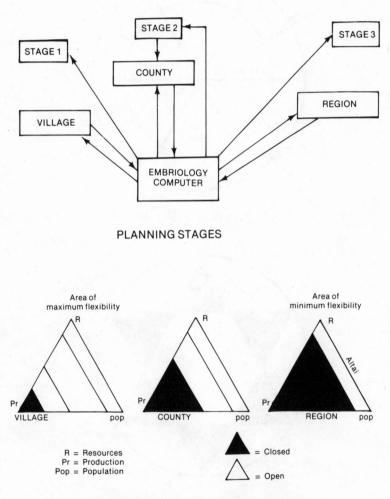

PLANNING STAGES

R = Resources
Pr = Production
Pop = Population

◆ = Closed

◇ = Open

DETERMINACY-INDETERMINACY RANGE

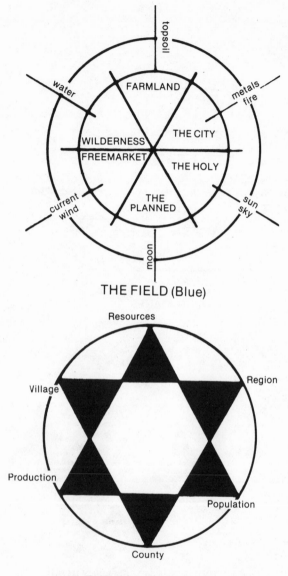

THE FIELD (Blue)

THE POINTS (Yellow)

A PROJECTED FILM

Alvarez would like to do a film on regional planning in Altai. But he has no time for it. He, Blake, and Morris are engaged by the Yellow shamans in their vaudeville show, which tours country fairs.

Still — Alvarez thinks about the film. How could such a film be made, taking into account the difficulties? (The complexity of the Embriology Computer, the feedback/feed-forward method of planning in Altai, etc.)

The Cuban sees two possibilities. The first would be a documentary approach: to show how the process actually works. It would be made up of interviews between the agents at the various levels explaining their roles: the matriarchs who operate the village consoles; the cauga or county planners collaborating with the village to put together the five-year plan; state and regional review boards, etc.

These nets would be concerned with examining the three basic terms of planning: agricultural and industrial production, the availability of natural resources, and population demands, and bringing them into balance. The entire *range* of subject matter would be indicated in a kind of cinematic shorthand: a film sequence of pastureland to denote resources. A scene from a steel mill or a Machine Bank. Population problems suggested by a shot of a teeming neighborhood, undernourished children, etc. But this would hardly make an absorbing film.

The second possibility would be to dramatize the personal element. A series of portraits showing the process as it intersects individual lives. For instance: the matriarchs in the Masters' Studio, they are making the plan with representatives of the farmers' collective — a freshness, a rough authenticity to this...the plan is sent up to the county planners at a higher level. These are more professional, pride themselves on a more objective view, as they evaluate it with the other village plans...conflicts of interests, attitudes?

But would this be sufficiently comprehensive? Would it not emphasize personalities at the expense of the clarity of the whole?

47

Finally, is it possible to treat the subject of planning at all in terms of art (even a popular art like the cinema)? One might illustrate the procedure as a conceptual scheme (the bones). And dramatize the agents and protagonists (the flesh and blood). But neither get at the interesting question about planning— whether in real life its direction runs from the top down, or from the bottom up. Who is the plan *for*?

In this regard Alvarez might film *two* possible ideal models for the country of Nghsi-Altai. One would be: maximum participation at the workplace and maximum local autonomy, within the framework of a central and binding macroeconomic plan (socialist model). The other that of overall production and distribution regulated by the play of global market forces; while at the same time brakes are applied to counter uneven development: the stunting of those areas which have nothing or little to offer in exchange (capitalist model).

But both models might be false. Could the art of the film show whether the plan were truth or fabrication?

But art is itself a fabrication.

• •

How to get below the surface?

One of the shamans suggests how Alvarez might solve the difficulty. Why not simply film the sequence of "Planning Dances" that are performed in Altai on Gobardan, during the Festival of Planners?

REGIONAL PLANNING DANCES: A SHAMAN'S DESCRIPTION

On the first day of Gobardan when the wheat yellows, the dances begin on the threshing floor of Sawna village. The year-end inventory has been made up by the Guild of Planners and a draft plan for the coming year forwarded to the county or cauga. It is the response of the county that initiates the dance series.

A CALENDAR

FIRST DANCE HOUSE   October 1
Village asking plan sent/answering plan received.
A.M.   March of the guild masters from the Studio of Planners.
P.M.   First Dance House by the villagers. Village dances. Reception of The Other.
That evening the panchayat in full assembly debates the options presented. Return to the Planners' Studio. Submission of second asking plan.

SECOND DANCE HOUSE   October 10
A.M.   March. Reception by the guild masters of the village — county answering plan.
P.M.   Barley threshing and bagging. Second Dance House by villagers. County dances. Reception of The Other.
Sequence of events morning afternoon, and evening, as described above.

THIRD DANCE HOUSE   October 24
A.M.   March, etc. Guild masters present the village-county-region answering plan.
P.M.   Wheat threshing and bagging. Third Dance House, Regional dances. Reception of The Other.
Sequence of events as before.

FOURTH DANCE HOUSE   November 10
A.M.   March. Presentation of village-county-region-confederacy answering plan.

P.M. Wheat threshing. The Fate Dances. Fourth Dance House.
In the evening, panchayat debates and final plan is decided.
Coded by the planners and fed into Embriology Computer.

NOVEMBER 11   FIRST DAY OF THE NEW YEAR
Afternoon: Transformation dances by the villagers: Fate dances
    continued. The Mysteries.
Evening: Announcement of confederacy-wide results.

SUGGESTED FILM SHOTS/TYPICAL START OF THE DAY

Note: during the course of each holiday all the villagers become
"planners," that is, they move away from the personal realm.
Perhaps a film sequence should show a typical family rising in the
morning. They wander around the house lazily. Perhaps one is
playing a flute; the clan is having breakfast...In a desultory way
they pull on their regalia, attach their tribal decorations and
feathers. And are *drawn* gradually out...first by the music of the
other villagers, the flutes the drums, heard in the lane. The sound
of the dancing in the lanes...very gradually swells...the excitement builds. The pull toward the threshing floor...

HEXAGON DANCES/GAMES

The threshing floor has become a hexagon, the space divided
roughly into six segments. On receiving the plan options, the participants dance as members of their phratries or brotherhoods.
    For instance, the Filtheater clans try to pull in the direction of
"Free Market"; the Soreheads toward "The Ruler/Full Moon,"
etc. (Suggested film shot number 2.)
    This is called "Moving the plan into one's corner." Thus the
saying in Altai: "The plan is pulled apart by the Six Tendencies."

MUSIC

Informal or random. Instruments of the participants, guitar, bagpipes, etc.

Formal, antiphonal. Two brass ensembles, one on each side of the threshing floor. Loud, brassy. Each band is under the direction of a shaman society.

MODES

Each Dance House is performed in two modes or moods. Mode of the dance is first comic, gross, ribald. The *low* planning or "kyogen dances."

At the appearance of The Other, the mode is satirical; then changes to grave and solemn. *High* planning style or "hinoh dances."

The participant is transformed through the modes.

MASKS/COSTUMES/REGALIA

First day: Rustic figures, lampoons, caricatures.
Second day: Animals and birds.
Third day: Insects and Regional Beings—rivers, mountains, etc.
Fourth day: Personification of weathers (confederacy-wide).

MEANING OF THE OTHER

In the middle of each festival dance, dividing the low and high modes, appears the Beggar. The figure is at first alien, in a different mask from the dancers. But at the start of the next Dance House, all wear this mask.

The Beggar does not represent the plan on a higher level (which would be merely an abstraction) but some other *place* or group that has hitherto been excluded. The Beggar dances as "Appala-chia," for example.

The Beggar is at first jeered at but later is "worshipped."

Sometimes the Beggar is not a representational figure but real. (Suggested film shot number 3.)

TRANSFORMATION DANCES/FATE DANCES

The dance houses essentially are the process by which the individual citizen transforms himself, that is, goes to meet his "developmental fate." This he does not do willingly, but neither is it unwilling either.

"I respond in order that I may change, and in order that I may be changed," is the saying in Altai.

The Beggar stands at the creode, or branching pathway. Sometimes one avoids him (goes around him). Sometimes one annihilates him. Sometimes one becomes him. In any case, one closes a door as one moves forward. This is why the last Dance Houses are called Fate Dances.

• •

After the planning dances are over, the panchayat decides the plan options in the full assembly of the people. Decision is by consensus. After that the plan is coded and submitted to the Embriology Computer. Thus it is said: "The village votes by counting heads and seeing faces. The confederacy votes by algebra."

Another one of our sayings in Altai: "The professional prepares/the dancer indicates/the panchayat acts."

However, the acts are not always virtuous. In deciding options the panchayat may chose either the "high" or the "low" mode.

• •

With the final mysteries and exchange of masks between the shaman societies—called the "marriage of shamans"—the New Year begins.

NEW YEAR'S NIGHT

A crew of shamans is filming the village New Year festivities. The scene is commonplace; and after six weeks of activities, during which many of the citizens have been dancing and arguing almost continually, the pace is slow. Therefore it is not an important film. Still, the film involves documenting and recording what is there; that is, replicating. It is only the Yellow shamans who are allowed to make films in Nghsi-Altai.

It is evening, but there is a full moon. There is sufficient moonlight to shoot the film. Besides, lights shine over the threshing floor. The screen of the Embriology Computer, set up at the edge of the field against the wall of the cannery, is also a source of light.

The same projection on similar screens is being shown in a thousand villages through Altai. The last deliberations have been taken simultaneously throughout the country, the choices made and programmed for the computer by the planners. The final returns are beginning to appear on the screen. In this village, as in a thousand other villages and city quarters as well, is being shown in flickering light the shape of the New Year.

The options have narrowed to one. The points or nodes of the branching pathways — once opened almost to infinity — have been danced through. Now the doors are closed. Flickering on the screen, in a pattern of shifting and changing equations and symbols: the cold light of the real.

This is the "blue light of balance" focused in a single finality by the planning process.

"We are awaiting our fate."

It is this mood that the shaman filmmakers are capturing.

A great heap of grain as high as the cannery roof stands under a lamp. The threshers and electric winnowing fans have been put away and the ground swept. There are some boys of the Squirrel or Naming Society sitting on a pile of pumpkins beside a parked truck. Others of the folk are sitting around eating New Year black millet and mung beans and drinking corn liquor.

On the threshing floor there is only a scattering of dancers. There are some musicians also. These are the hardiest and most perservering dances. Their faces gleam with sweat and their arms and legs are white with chaff.

Two old sendi drinkers are weaving among the dancers. It is not clear whether they are trying merely to cross the space or to perform on it. One has a limp bagpipe under his arm which he blows fornlornly.

Voices call: "Sit down, Harelip. What are you trying to do?"

"Time to go home, Uncle Desai. You haven't any breath left."

A wind has sprung up, whirling the chaff. Beyond the granary. bins and over the shoulder of the windmill, the moon is sailing. Heads are turned upward. From the great screen there is a wash of light turning the faces of the onlookers blue.

A family of a dozen or so — the Harditt family, perhaps — is sitting near the film crew around a picnic hamper. A small girl is on her mother's lap. As the figures on the screen move and flicker, she tries to keep her eyes open, fighting sleep.

Is this Lucia's child?

THE POPULATION LOTTERY

The final returns are known. The plan is made, through the network of communication and consultation and through the Embriology Computer. Now it must be acted upon.

"Technology is a tool. But the tool is iron."

Each commune must live within its "force triangle" composed of the three vectors:

PRODUCTION/RESOURCES/POPULATION

In some distant sections of Nghsi-Altai there has been drought. The monsoon rains have not come in season. And this burden must be distributed through every part. To keep the balance, the Sawna families will be diminished.

In Sawna it was the Nai headsman (the rites master) who presided over the population lottery. This was held in the square in front of the baithak a week after New Year. The actual drawing took place on the baithak porch. On the dusty ground below stood the folk. Families had come in from the other cauga villages, from Rampur and Dabar Jat. Clansmen from the "daughter villages," that is, those with blood ties, had also returned to Sawna for the lottery drawing.

On a table on the porch was a large jar full of dried yellow beans. There was also a scattering of black beans. The lottery drawing was no different from any other lottery drawing — for instance, the choosing of officials, or factory managers in the machine banks of the cauga. Blue shamans' weeds decorated the railing of the baithak porch.

It was the old women — the heads of each family — that reached into the jar and pulled out a bean. They came out of the crowd with dark reluctance — it was almost as if they were being *pulled* out of it, like turnips out of the ground — while the knots of relatives that surrounded them pulled at their shawls making a great show of refusing to let them go forward. Finally they did so and were escorted with great dignity up the steps to the platform by the rites master.

However, it was not the matriarch herself who would be sent away if her selection were unlucky. In a ritual sense the whole clan was marked, but in practice it was only "second generation's households" that would be forced to leave Sawna. Not the family community—only a part torn out and sent into exile beyond the borders—like the thinning of forest trees.

At the bottom of the baithak steps, members of the Dog Society lounged and played dominos. In the small shade of a banana plantation, a hookah smoking group was in progress, the old men occasionally shifting their places to avoid the sun.

It was Helvetia Harditt who picked the black bean.

FAREWELL TO SAWNA VILLAGE

The sun shone on a white wall. Venu was wakened by a cart clattering over the cobbles. Sathan lay against him.

A pot banged in the kitchen. He heard someone cry: "You there, get me those eggs." Helvetia's voice continued: "I'm letting them sleep. The packing is mostly done anyway."

And another voice: "Yes, they have a long day ahead of them. Let them rest."

Most of the other occupants at the sleeproom had already gotten up. Venu noted that his son, Dhillon, who had spent the night with his extended family, was gone. Maddi and her husband lay still asleep. But Lucia's children were up already, their bedrolls piled neatly against the wall.

Where were they? Dhillon may have taken the boy and girl to the pasture on a last visit, Venu thought. Someone would have to be sent to fetch them or they might be left behind.

Venu pictured Harelip with his load of pumpkins bound for the freeze locker and the little mare on a lead trotting beside its mother as she pulled the cart. As the cart turned a corner, the clattering diminished but the light twinkling bell attached to the mare's harness continued clear.

Yes, for the last time, Venu thought.

The sleeping gallery was almost empty. The part of the floor where they lay was still in shadow. An oblong of light washed across the wall where a lacrosse racket hung twisted with a knot of dry grass from Watermeadow.

Again, voices from the kitchen.

He could hear Nanda's and Motteram's voices arguing sharply.

Sathan's face was blurred as she lay resting on her husband's brown arm. Venu had thought she was asleep, but she was not. As he pushed her hair aside, gently so as not to waken her, he could see that she was awake. The daily sounds of the house floated up. And Sathan lay without moving listening to them, her eyes filled with tears.

Lucia's children, Bhungi and Lal, accompanied by two uncles, were going on a walk outside the village. They were going to say good-bye to the herdsmen.

The uncles, Dhillon and one of the city-dwelling Harditts, would also be bidding the children good-bye.

Dhillon, who had arrived from his in-law village the day before, was explaining the mysteries of the Motor and Metals Pool to the city relative. Leaving the village outskirts they struck out across the fields. The older men had set out on their walk in a somber mood, each holding a child by the hand. Now however, lost in conversation, they had forgotten them.

The uncles walked ahead rapidly. Dhillon occasionally stopped to point out something remembered from his herdsman's days, then resumed the climb with long strides. The pylons of the power lines marching up the middle of the pasture had been decorated with tantras during Dasahra, he recalled. By that stone wall the cowherds had built their fire in winter. The children struggled to keep up.

A truck loaded with its clanking field kitchen climbed by them slowly along the road which marked the edge of the canefield. The field was now stubble, stretching as far as the eye could see.

Over a rise they came on a band of young herders. Around the margin of the water hole the grass was green, but beyond it was straw. The mild-eyed cattle, the color of coffee, grazed at a distance. A herdsman was playing an accordion.

At the bottom on the gently sloping hill lay the village, and on this side of the village the wash pond.

After a while one of the men stood up and came over to the children, who were occupying themselves catching grasshoppers. Then another man came over. Lal had a grasshopper cupped in his fist. Struggling to get out, it tickled.

"So. You'll be going away from us?"

Bhungi nodded with an air of importance. "Yes. Today." The smaller Lal also nodded.

"Where will you be going?"

Bhungi swung her arm vaguely. "To America."

Through the windbreak of locust trees they could see where the women were washing clothes at the edge of the pond.

By mid-morning their travel guides had come. The two households leaving to go on the long trip through Kansu Hardan had packed, and the children had been collected. They said good-bye to the others, left the house where they had lived as long as they could remember, and closed the gate.

Neighbors stood in the doorways of the lane watching them as they passed. The robing ceremony had been the day before, and the formal family farewell at the Ancestor shrine. Helvetia Harditt representing the Lineage, the line of the family through time, had said the prayer and given them mementos from the altar to carry with them. Jeth Harditt on behalf of each of the "in-law" villages throughout the district had also said a few words.

The Blue priest Tattattatha had also taken part in the melancholy ceremony.

Now they walked through the lane of the tholla in their exile robes. The children had been given yucca blossoms, which they held tightly in their fists. The procession was quiet, accompanied only by the shamans' rattles. In the doorway a woman with a child leaning against her took it onto her lap and clutched it tightly. The pair, mother and child, watched the procession pass with cold eyes. Already a shadow seemed to have passed over them.

Several other exile families had gathered in the square. The collection crossed Maker's Square and went up the ramp onto the vegetable gardens. The sun was shining on the pale aster flowers below the hedges. The stucco wall of a cottage was covered with red henna hand marks, for a wedding. In fact, at the village gate a bridegroom, his head capped with silver bells and his ankles jangling, passed them on a motorcycle.

He slowed down and waved.

A small crowd of villagers had followed the exile families as far as the common orchards. Then they went through the gate and were crossing the fields alone, accompanied only by the Yellow shamans.

• •

In the villages adjacent to Sawna there had been no additions to the caravans of lottery losers. However, out of the four-village cluster comprising the next cauga they had picked up three families, and in the next shire several more.

For some days the exile caravan continued over the plain. They would stop every night and pitch camp outside a village. These villages, dug into the loess earth, were the same as their own. The wayfarers were seldom more than three miles from a village. Yet only the roofs with their warm colors and a few guild halls and windmills could be seen. In front of these the heat shimmered, heightening the atmosphere of impermanence and distance.

The Sawna people were drifting. And it was an unsettling thought that even the soil in which the Jat villages were anchored had drifted in from the desert millenia ago. Was the landscape again shifting? However, life within the villages continued as normal, heedless of the border-bound travelers.

To the Harditt contingent it seemed strange that for years there had been these moving caravans of exiles and they had hardly noticed them. They had passed outside the walls, shepherded by the shamans. Perhaps it was the influence of the Yellow shamans that erased the fact of their passing.

Though there was no formal organization, the sections of the caravan tended to correspond to the "bisa cauga," the twenty-village unit or cluster of the plains region. The Sawna pilgrims marched with others, were part of the same slow-moving baggage train, and often shared the same vehicle, a tractor or lumbering bullock cart. These were generally overloaded. Indeed, some of the "second-generation" families had taken along household equipment and even their draft animals.

The Harditts watched one family approach over the fields — a truck piled high with bundles, on top of which rode a grandmother and a crate of chickens.

"It's as if they think they're going to a new settlement. And can start all over again, planting their own yam patch," Nanda remarked humorously to Golla.

Maddi, who was pregnant, took turns with a young woman from Sawna with an infant, riding on a cart and walking. Ramdas, Maddi's husband, walked beside them.

• •

One afternoon the Sawna people had pitched camp. The children had scampered off with friends they had made in the caravan.

After a short while Lal and Bhungi were back. Bhungi tugged at her father's sleeve excitedly.

"Come. There's a dead animal."

Since they had arrived a sickly sweet smell had pervaded the campsite. The clan people were setting up yurts. As they approached the village ditch they could see birds settling on the trees. The stench increased. The pasture, cropped close, was stippled with splotches of pink thistles.

On the flat ground at about a hundred yards distant lay a dead bullock. The animal was on its side, its body against the earth stiff, its four legs sticking straight out. The head was wedged back. A single kite perched between the horns. They were too far away to see whether the eyes had been eaten yet by the birds.

Other birds stood in a dignified pose or stepped slowly over the body. The glossy black hide was distended but still intact. The birds were mostly kites, with one or two white long-necked egrets.

There was a tranquility about the birds, particularly the egrets. They simply stood pruning their feathers or bent down to pick for skin parasites as they had before on the live ox. Perhaps they did not realize yet that the animal was really dead and not merely lying down resting.

At the rear, heavily, a carrion hawk dropped down and began ripping at once at the bullock's anus. There was a stir among the birds on the body. As if with a shock, they too began to pull violently at the carcass.

A sober assembly of egrets and kites watched at a short distance from the corpse. The trees at the edge of the field were now thick with birds.

Lal almost overcome with nausea put his sleeve over his nose and clung to his father. Bhungi wanted to get closer.

Shamans came onto the pasture. The travelers could not tell whether they were from the village or were the same shamans as those in charge of the caravan, as they also were muffled against the stench. Their heads were covered. They were wearing heavy gloves. They stepped through the parliament of birds.

One of the shamans knocked the strutting birds away with his stick. They poured gasoline over the corpse.

These shamans were knackers, Motterman told Bhungi. In the old days their task had been to prepare leather. Their customers had been the villagers, but because the task was unclean they were not allowed inside the village.

The sky was still white as the Sawna folk went down the road and after they had returned to camp. They could see the smoke from the burning corpse a long time, and in the distance other wavering columns of smoke where the shamans were probably burning other dead cattle.

• •

Venu's daughter was having trouble balancing on top of the weaving baggage. Articles from the ancestor shrine were also loaded onto the truck. From a pole decorated with photographs, a black streamer drifted against Maddi's face.

Both Maddi and her father had been on this same route before with the old councilor, Gopal Harditt. Since they had left the village and had been taken from the compound, Venu had felt intensely the presence of the former panchayat head.

Venu and Ramdas were plodding along beside the truck. Every so often Maddi's young husband would reach up and touch the pregnant woman's leg or hand. A shaman walked a few steps in front of the group.

From the fringes of the Yellow shaman's shirt hung all manner of clinking charms and trinkets. Had the shaman also known Gopal Harditt? Venu wondered. The Yellow shamans were connected to the Ancestor societies. Did not the shamans guide the "most recent dead," just as they were the travel guides of the exiles?

The caravan route was through a familiar landscape. Nor was traveling with the caravan strange, as it swelled with new additions from the provincial villages. The dress and articles of regalia showing the Age Grades were alike throughout Kansu. The elders were accorded their proper rank. The brotherhoods with their characteristic tattoos could also be distinguished easily.

The Harditt men struck up an acquaintance with members of Wind clan from the village of Ladpur and with several Firemen. During the intermittent halts they would sit and smoke together in the shade of a truck. Sometimes they would play bowls.

The treeless road continued. The caravan generally halted early at a watering place outside some village bounds. The creak and sway of the loads ceased. The riders clambered down stiffly. Soon over the open field one could see the circles of the yurts going up and the smoke rising from the first cooking fires.

WITH THE TRAVELING SHOW

For a stretch of the journey they fell in with the traveling show. It had been performing on a riverbank on the outskirts of Puth Majra where a fair was being held. The shamans' troupe, which projected movies and gave dramatic entertainment, was also traveling through the villages of the Kansu district.

Toward the end of each day the members of the exile caravan would pick their campsite and be busy setting up their shelters. Nearby on the same pasture they would see the players erecting their bamboo platform and hanging up their ragged screen.

The platform for the performance was set outside the limits of the village, and the villagers came out to it, often bringing their campstools. Because it was beyond the village bounds the exiles also were permitted to attend the showings.

The shaman troupe practiced their dance steps on the grass beside the parked trucks. The shamans took different "voices." Sometimes in the evenings the campers could hear them practicing with their voices on the hill or under the orchard trees. They could project their voices so that they seemed to come from another place or out of another person's mouth.

The three foreigners attached to the troupe also practiced. They specialized in acrobatics and juggling feats and performed their "individuality freak shows." These took place during the intermission and were in the nature of a comic relief to the more sober spirit dramas.

The Sawna folk had seen many Yellow shamans' shows. In the performance an ordinary villager, called simply "Man" or "Person," goes on a journey, is captured and taken to the land of the dead, or Under world. There one of the spirit animals befriends him and becomes his Spirit Helper, giving him its own powers. The person then returns to the village and shows his magic.

There are a number of demonstrations of skill. One of the shaman dancers reaches with his fingers into a boiling kettle and eats a piece of meat out of it. A cornstalk is made to sprout before the eyes of spectators and produce a fully ripened ear of corn.

The shamans contain inside them the spirit animals, whose presence may be manifested by kicks and other signs. Once a horse was inside one shaman's body, and whenever a certain song was sung the horse tried to get out and the audience could see the horse's tail protruding from the dancer's mouth.

The Sawna spectators enjoyed these "demonstrations of powers." Some were less impressed. Motteram described them as "cheap conjurer's tricks." Generally it was the younger men who were inclined to be skeptical of the shamans' exhibitions, which they found grotesque. They preferred the more civilized Dance Houses of the Blue shamans.

It was true that the magic of the Yellow shamans shows tended to wear off. The Sawna householders had seen them many times. They had somewhat lost their effect.

Several days before someone had lost a wallet. One of the shaman guides had helped find it. The shamans guiding the caravan also it seemed had special powers—like their cousins the performers in the shows.

The wallet, belonging to a family from the bisa cauga, had been lost en route several days before. People had looked for it everywhere, and the shaman, through his "third eye," had located it under a certain bush in a previous camp. They had gone back and found it. This shaman had been traveling with their section, and the Harditts had walked with him often. How was it possible to see things that were not there?

The shaman explained that the third eye was a three-foot-long tube he imagined protruding from his head, formed of rays of light which he was able to focus on the lost object.

Now a circle of campers was gathered around the same shaman, whose name was Elwood. The group included Nanda and two grandchildren.

This time the shaman was giving a "spirit reading" for a dog. The dog belonged to a friend of Lal's. The owner sat holding the dog, and the shaman sat across from the two of them chewing betel nut.

As the dog was present in the flesh it was not necessary for the shaman to use his "third eye." He was in direct communication with the spirit, and the dog spoke through his mouth.

Like all shamans this one had poor eyesight. He complained that the light bothered him. Shielding his eyes he squinted into the faces of the persons questioning him without seeming to see them.

He seemed to be seeing the small child and her dog only vaguely.

After the seance Elwood was asked about the dog's "aura." He explained that the aura was not very strong, not like the aura of a person, because the colors are not as bright. There is a lemon yellow which in the aura of an animal denotes affection. And a blue color which shows the energy flow of all spirits.

Did he see other colors in these astral emanations?

Yes, a wide band of green. That is the healing force that animals give out, particularly when a child has been sick.

Nanda asked the shaman whether he could see also the auras of trees and stones? Sathan and Lucia were beside her.

"Of course. Everything in nature."

"Even small things? A flea's aura?"

The shaman nodded. "And you will see them too."

• •

The rawhide costumes were a product of the shamans' "knacker" activity. They would sew onto it beads, hammered pieces of metal, bird feathers, and bits of shell in the old manner. The leather was caked with grime. The raffia costumes of the theatrical performers were less durable but cleaner. Occasionally they had to be completely remade; then the caravan people would be sent out into the field to cut straw and to bring it in in bundles. The children brought feathers.

Most entrancing were the rattles. These were called "thunder sticks" and were made out of gourds filled with pebbles. The fringes of the shamans' garments also sounded: with the rattling of claws, deer hooves, the beaks of owls and clapper rails, etc.

The masks were of animals and birds, even fish and insects, which represented the clan totems. Made of hides and carved wood, they were double and triple masks, with the features painted inside and out so that they could be seen also when the masks were open.

Once Lal was taken over to the performers' camp by his grandfather and permitted to sit on the lap of one of the shamans. The double mask was held up and the little boy taught how to open and close it by pulling the thong.

The Westerners, Blake, Morris, and Alvarez, who were practicing nearby, had stopped to watch the demonstration.

• •

One evening the Sawna households had been watching the flickering movie screen from a distance. In order to see better the children stood on a wagon.

Then the shaman dances began. Motteram suggested they get closer.

"Not in front," Ramdas warned. They were under an array of generator poles. An eerie light fell from above in the direction of the dancers.

The men made their way across the slope at the backs of the spectators and came in toward the corner of the stage to the side. From this vantage the Sawna people could see both the stage and the backstage performers readying themselves to go on and pulling on their costumes. The Shaman musicians, three on each side, squatted at the edge of the stage before their instruments, which were drums and rattles. There was also a storyteller.

A man appeared, walking. Perhaps he was going off from the village to fish.

A creature bounded on. This was the cannibal bird, Bakbakwalanusiwa, the storyteller announced in his whining voice. The body of the actor was partly hidden under straw thatch. The ferocious head was mounted on top of his own. With his hands he operated the long beak decorated with eye and nose holes.

The villager was taken to the land of the dead, to Under world. But where is the land of the dead? Is it below ground or above it? Voices come to us from Under world, but from where?

Stretching out its wings the being threw a larger and even more

68

menacing shadow against the canvas. The whining voice rose. The Sawna men leaning against the edge of the stage could feel against their chests and hands the pounding of the dancing feet. The bird's bony ankles rattled. The figure loomed over them with its hooked beak.

There were in fact three creatures. The spotted muzzle of Hyena opened, the jaws swung apart. Bear's faced showed below, lazy and crafty. The dance tempo increased. Finally this mask was pulled sideways. With a shiver the spectators perceived Spirit Being appear, with his beak of bone and eyes gleaming, made out of scintillating blue shells.

Though there were only two actors, there appeared to be many, and it was awesome. It was as if the shaky bamboo platform, so plain and unimpressive looking during the day, had become at night a field of force. The dancers were possessed by the animal and spirit beings — and at same time *were* the animal and spirit beings.

However, when the dance was over, and when the performer stepped from the side of the stage and took off his mask — the Sawna men saw he was the familiar shaman. He was the same person, now somewhat exhausted, that had been standing next to them as he adjusted his costume only a few minutes before.

It was not the same with the three foreigners, who performed next. They did not dance using the generalized animal or bird masks, but as individuals. In fact they wore the masks of their own faces. The masks were perhaps exaggerated. The pallor of the skin, the prominent noses, and deeply recessed eye sockets of the Westerners gave them a ghostly quality. As the figures danced there seemed to be *only* the masks and costumes. Through the eyeholes of the masks the Sawna men, from their vantage point at the edge of the stage, were astonished to see nothing, only a kind of smokey vagueness.

Were the Westerners' spirits entangled in the shamans' coat fringes? If so, where had they come form? From Under world, storehouse of souls?

The Sawna men watched closely.

When the Morris and Blake figures came off the stage the performers had actually dematerialized. It took several minutes for their bodies to reappear.

• •

Venu, Rathlee Golla, and Motteram, coming to pay their friends a last visit, found the foreigners behind a tent. The battered truck, with the name of the troupe painted on the side, was parked nearby. Theatrical paraphernalia spilled out of it. The Westerners had been doing their washing. Articles of clothing, mostly old socks and underwear, were strung on a line.

This was the lottery losers' last stop in Kansu. After that, the caravan was scheduled to go on into another province, while the players continued to tour the villages.

The stopover at this campsite had been for several days— longer than usual—enabling the foreigners to catch up on their housekeeping.

The Sawna men squatted. Between the truck and the tent, the ground was worn bare where the players had been practicing. Morris, his arms covered with suds, bent over a basin.

Motteram, though he had been afraid of him at first, had grown particularly fond of Alvarez. All the Westerners were pink, but Alvarez was the pinkest and most flamboyant. His hair stuck out angrily from his head like a hive of bees. The missing ears with their patches of scar tissue heightened this effect of ferocity.

However, at the moment it seemed the fire had gone out of him. The filmmaker sat disconsolately on the ground mending his socks.

In the vaudeville skit the Cuban socialist gives a long and pathetic description of how he came to the country as an explorer, married, and worked in a noodle factory. He is asked by one of the shamans how he lost his ears. Alvarez replies:

> I am lucky I did not lose my hand
>> meddling in the economy of this country
> I would have had all of you stamping out machine products
>> and tied to a production line
> With no room to breathe.

This is said so penitently and with such an air of injured inno-
cence—the eyes rolled up and the hand held over his head in a
gesture of surprise—it makes the audience laugh.

In fact, the confession was false. As Alvarez himself had been
at pains to point out to Motteram and to anyone else who would
listen, he had been misunderstood. He had not been interested in
the assembly line but rather in increasing the country's general
abundance and well-being. But such was his sinister role in the
theatrical performance, whenever he appeared he was hissed—
proof of his guilt being his mutilated ears.

Unlike Alvarez, Morris's routine was not set. He composed the
songs himself and generally went over them late in the afternoon
before each performance. He had finished rinsing and running his
articles through the wringer. As he hung them on the clothesline,
Morris sang to himself softly:

> I who have loved old things
>   old crafts   old trappings
> looked for them in a new land
>   with no routes   no mappings
>
> I did not seek them in art—the dyer's color
>   the fine line
>   incised by the smith on his silver
> but in the product's wholeness   a sense of measure
>   that joined maker and user
>
> I found them best in the songs
>   the ancient artifacts of this place
>   and your deepest treasure
> And you have called me a thief of songs
>   and put me in shackles.

He paused. Inadvertently Morris reached down and rubbed his
ankle where he had been held in the stocks.

Rathlee asked with sympathy, "Do you still suffer pain?"

The poet-artist, a bluff, forthright man, had struck Venu and

71

Golla as the most approachable of the three. And perhaps he had suffered most. He had committed one of the gravest crimes, to have taken down music sung by the folk, on a tape-recorder— thus pre-empting the right of the Yellow shamans to replicate.

"Well, I've learned my lesson at any rate. Nothing is set. One must compose extempore, in life as in art, depending on one's mood and circumstance."

He sang again—in a revision of the last stanza:

> In your foreign land
>   how we are marked!
> How strange
>   that our deepest passions
> should be for you
>   mere eccentricities.

"Yes, things alter," Rathlee Golla said. "Perhaps everything... The song, the man, the landscape, it's all a trick of perspective."

Venu was sitting on the ground. The others watched him in silence as he finished weaving a figure out of blades of kana grass. He finished the bird. He attached a handle to the bird's neck, made out of the same spiky grass, pulled at it with the back of his knife, and curled it. He presented it to Morris.

"And what about him?" Rathlee asked, pointing to a figure on the stage.

Morris laughed. "Oh him. He has a madman's role to play!"

It was still an hour before the performance. Blake had mounted the platform and was practicing some of his stage business.

Blake's shirtfront was open, showing a flowing cravat. He wore high boots and an American cavalry hat. His suit was composed of pantaloons and a knee-length coat, both of loud black-and-white striped worsted. The large nose and closely set eyes with deep eyefolds were the only features visible in a bloom of wiry white hair.

Some shamans in the field were putting up the loudspeaker equipment. Already the performer had a few impromptu spec-

72

tators among the campers. There was a scattering of applause as Blake stepped forward and adjusted the microphone. "Can you hear me back there?" He struck a bardic pose.

"I shall begin with a little warmup. What I call my inflationary verses."

He took a deep breath and began:

> "I celebrate myself....
> I loaf and write my soul,
> I lean and loaf at my ease observing a spear
> of summer grass."

"My god, it's not his own poem!" Alvarez exclaimed. He and Morris had stepped over to watch. "He's expropriating another's verses!"

"And misquoting at that. No matter," Morris reassured him. "So long as he sticks to the repertory of Egotism."

> "...the smoke of my own breath
> echoes, ripples and buzzed whispers...
> my respiration and inspiration...
> ...the passing of blood and air through my lungs,
> the songs of ME rising from bed and meeting the sun."

There were cries of encouragement from the audience. The poet continued more volubly.

> "Swift wind! Space! My soul!
> Divine I am inside and out, I make holy whatever
> I touch or am touched from
> The scent of these arm-pits is an aroma finer
> than prayer....
> Seeing, hearing and feeling are miracles, and each
> part and tag of me is a miracle."

A dreamy look of contentment settled on the poet's face.

"I dote on myself....
I sing the body electric
I have instant conductors all over me whether I
    pass or stop
They seize every object....

I hear you whispering there O stars of heaven
    perpetual transfers....
I ascend from the moon, I ascend from the night....
Wrenched and sweaty....
The spotted hawk swoops by....
I am not a bit tamed, I too am unstranslatable,
I SOUND MY BARBARIC YAWP OVER THE ROOFS OF
    THE WORLD."

There was by this time a swell of prolonged applause and hand-clapping from the handful of camp followers at the foot of the stage, as Blake had continued to the end with mounting fervor.

They clamored for another.

"I hope it will be his — but I wouldn't count on it," Morris said to Alvarez in an aside.

"Here's one of my more recent compositions, in a darker mood." Blake threw his head back. His forehead had grown purple. He started off the text, shouting, at top speed.

MOLOCH THE INCOMPREHENSIBLE PRISON!... MOLOCH THE VAST
    STONE OF WAR! MOLOCH OF STUNNED GOVERMENTS!....
MOLOCH WHOSE EYES ARE A THOUSAND BLIND WINDOWS!
    MOLOCH WHOSE SKYSCRAPERS STAND IN THE LONG STREETS
    LIKE ENDLESS JEHOVAHS! MOLOCH WHOSE FACTORIES
    DREAM AND CROAK IN THE FOG! MOLOCH WHOSE
    SMOKESTACKS AND ANTENNAE CROWN THE CITIES!
MOLOCH IN WHOM I SIT LONELY! MOLOCH IN WHOM I DREAM
    ANGELS. CRAZY IN MOLOCH! COCKSUCKER IN MOLOCH!
    LACKLOVE AND MANLESS IN MOLOCH!
MOLOCH! MOLOCH! ROBOT APARTMENTS! INVISIBLE SUBURBS!
    SKELETON TREASURIES! BLIND CAPITALS! DEMONIC

INDUSTRIES! SPECTRAL NATIONS! INVINCIBLE
MADHOUSES! GRANITE COCKS! MONSTROUS BOMBS!

"He dearly loves to howl," Morris remarked to the Sawna men. "And this is only the warmup. Can you imagine how he's going to take off on the night session!"

Blake was introducing his next offering, which he called "A Vision."

"Ah, the authentic Blake! But no doubt to be badly mangled."

The poet began:

"A new heaven is begun. And as it is now thirty-three years since its advent, the Eternal Hell revives.

"The prophets Isaiah and Ezekiel dined with me amid the fires of hell. Both roundly asserted — and in this I concur — that the ancient tradition that the world will be consumed in fire at the end of six thousand years is true.

"Already the fountain of fire overflows and the secret world — chinked by our senses five — is exposed.

"Rintrah roars and swags on the angry deep.

"Shadow of prophecy, Albion's coast is sick; the American meadows faint!

"France, rend down thy dungeon! Golden Spain; burst the barriers of old Rome!

"The fire, the fire is falling! Look up, look up! O citizen of London, enlarge thy countenance! O Jew, leave counting gold! Return to thy oil and wine. O African, go winged thought, widen his forehead!

"The fierce limbs, the flaming hair, shot like the sinking sun into the western sea.

"The Eternal Female groans."

Blake was weeping at the end of these stanzas, and the audience was in a trance state.

Venu commented, "We find it strange, this vision of the future ...when here there is only present time."

Already Alvarez had wandered off. Morris returned to his

washing. The fire under the wash tub was low. The older man sent the children to fetch sticks.

Blake descended from the stage, spent. He was going among the spectators. He was coming toward them, his hands, loose, chewing a blade of grass.

But the audience was still in a state of excitement, warmed by fires that were in their own country illicit, of egotism, romantic challenge and scrappiness, and apocalyptic prophecy.

THE PICNIC WITH TATTATTATHA

The caravan passed the Great Sandy and Little Sandy rivers. Crossing over into Shao province, there had been behind them over the plain a last glimpse of the tall buildings and factories of Puth Majra. To the west there was a line of tawny mountains. These lay in the direction in which the Wind clansmen had once traveled on the way to Goose Gap and the tribal encampment at Watermeadow.

The caravan slowly crossed over a high gorge. They looked over into an abyss which was almost dry. The bridge, under repair, was supported by a tenuous bamboo scaffolding on which a team of roustabouts were at work. The Harditt men thought they recognized Dhillon's old companion, Rawilpindi.

Here the land was more arid. It was flatter, and there were irrigated sections. The route of the caravan paralleled a line of blue hills which neither receded nor came any closer. In this district the village clusters were more widely spaced. Each cluster yielded its lottery losers.

These new pilgrims were Luns. Their language was only partly comprehensible to the Jats, their gestures brusquer. But in build and color they were similar.

With the filling of the exile quotas from the rest of the plains districts, the caravan stretched out in a thin file along the road for several miles. It moved slowly.

Now, when in the late afternoon the Sawna group arrived at the outskirts of some village, the long caravan still moved up behind, the loaded trucks swung into view, and it would be almost night before the last yurts were pitched.

There were no more traveling shows. Sometimes in the dusk outside these villages a gathering of peasants stood watching the arrivals, beside a tractor.

•　•

Venu found himself annoyed with Sathan. His wife and daughter, who had been responsible for the Harditt packing, had each taken along an extra shawl but had neglected to bring his favorite mug for coffee.

Meanwhile Nanda was having a feud with Motteram. In the early stages of the journey, betel nut had been plentiful. One could walk up and down the caravan and see the old women chewing it, a look of relaxed contentment on their faces. Now the gums of the matriarchs were no longer stained purplish black. When Nanda stuck out her tongue, it was like a child's.

In the normal course of things she would have sent her son-in-law out to bargain or trade for the nuts. When Nanda ordered Motteram, he refused. As they no longer lived in the village he was free of his apprenticeship obligation.

Lucia sided with Motteram. The dispute was carried on vociferously for some nights — not in the bosom of the family but around the campfire with everybody watching. Indeed, the audience of outsiders made the controversy more ugly.

• •

The travels through Shao province continued. Lal and Bhungi roamed the caravan and the adjacent fields with the other children. The contingent from the Ladpur sixteen-villages or bisacauga tended to stick together on the road. At night they pitched camp, helping each other put up the yurts. Meals were shared and decisions of the improvised panchayat were taken around a common fire.

The cauga campsite was ordinarily laid out in the shape of an ellipse, with the sites occupied by the families around the periphery. If possible these were grouped according to tribe or tendency. Thus on one side of the Ladpur ellipse were the Tractor Operators and the Sliding Fish people and opposite them the Filtheaters and Soreheads. The Harditts were of this latter category (under the Moon sign) and regularly pitched their tent next to another family of Moons.

• •

Not far from the dusty road, Lal and Ramdas came across the skeleton of a bullock. The skull lay porous on the field. Only above the hooves were there meager tufts of hide. The bones had been plucked clean. Lal stood twisting on his finger a ring of sweet fern.

The whiteness and the cleanness were startling. There were only the light curving bones. The child's uncle would not let him touch the skeleton.

"Now it must be reclothed."

Lal's nose puckered. Ramdas explained that were was a storehouse under the ground for souls and that the species of beings in the world were constant and did not diminish.

When the child looked at him puzzled, Ramdas merely said: "You will see another ox walking."

Still, the matter continued to puzzle the child's youngest uncle. Did the teachings mean that in the Underworld storehouse, there was always the same *number* of souls? Or did it refer only to species—which remained constant though the numbers of individuals grew or diminished?

He discussed the question over glasses of sendi with his father-in-law and Rathlee Golla, and several other Fifth Age Set men. Ramdas was astonished to discover that each held a different opinion on the matter. Perhaps the question could have been resolved had there been a member of the Ancestor Society present.

• •

Tattattatha joined the Harditt group. The Blue Sensor, who had traveled without his leopard, relayed a number of messages from the Sawna compound. A Harditt cousin of Rathlee, of the Third Age Grade, was enrolled in the Weather and Soils Station. Sathan and Lucia were informed of progress at the Master's Studio. A new synthesizer had been installed, and they were preparing the printout of the autumn plan.

Sathan said, "Well, I guess they're getting along well enough without me."

"Does that surprise you?" Maddi countered.

After giving his news, Tattattatha made a tour of inspection around the campsite with the reigning matriarch, a Topsoil tribeswoman. The two walked with great dignity along the six boundaries dividing the space. Each segment was blessed with one of the "blue wilderness weeds."

• •

The hills were lower and had changed from smoky blue to slate. They had reached the last border settlement before the swamp

79

country. There was a grove of palm trees fronting an immense field where pineapples were grown. Along the side was a row of bright aluminum-clad cannery buildings. These were backed by a low dyke. Beyond, stretching as far as the eye could see, was a feathery wall of bamboo.

There had been canneries connected with the machine bank in Sawna, but these were larger. The line of bitaura-driven truck-carts, which shuttled back and forth from the fields to the processing shed, was also a familiar sight in Sawna.

Yet this was perhaps the last time they would be seeing the carts—and the fields and the agricultural settlement too. In fact these days, the Harditts reminded themselves, all sights were "for the last time."

• •

Tattattatha had spent the evening before at the encampment. After breakfasting with the others on millet cakes seasoned with catni and a cup of sit, he remarked that he would like to stretch his legs. Together with a number of county folk, he set out on a walk through the palm grove. The group included Sathan.

The sun had just risen and was barely over the horizon. The sandy ground under the coconut palms was a bright glitter. The trunks were dark, they strolled over the violet shadows.

The exile caravan from the plains biome was now complete. A thousand yurts—in clusters of half dozen to twenty—filled the grove which extended for half a mile along the edge of the pineapple plantation.

The yurt clusters or caugas were named after the counties from which the wayfarers had come. The encampment was thus a miniature region of the plains in exile. The clusters had been pitched the night before in the cool sand and would soon be taken down. In fact, the trucks and other vehicles which had transported the pilgrims thus far were being assembled preparatory to the trip back. Baggage was piled among the palm tree trunks, also to be returned. They passed several caugas where a Yellow shaman squatted on top the the piles, lazily smoking bhang.

A steady stream of strollers moved the length of tented grove viewing the assembly. Tattattatha passing another Blue shaman that he knew would exchange greetings, and they would make the "balancing" sign, touching each other first on both palms, then on the forearms.

Returning to the Ladpur cauga, they found their own folk already packing. A crowd gathered around Tattattatha. The priest, making the round of the yurts, appeared to be displeased. He pointed out that the sacred circle was incomplete. Two of the brotherhoods were missing.

Sathan, next to him, replied that among the lottery losers in their own county, there had been no Fire people or Sky clans chosen. "So naturally," Sathan added, "we set up the tents as we could. It is not our fault there are empty spaces."

Tattattatha, frowning, looked at the faces of the group crowded around him.

"I can see lots of masters, and people of the First, Third, Fourth, and Fifth Age Grades. But there are no Seconds, or any old people either. How can you make the journey without a commune?"

He selected people to fill the missing age grades and brotherhoods and coached them in their roles. The Blue priest spent the rest of the day, as he told them, reconstituting civil society.

•   •

The region of the plains was assembled by its caugas or counties. Each county, gathered around its Blue priest, was having its picnic in the immense pineapple field. This was the "passover" meal being celebrated.

The mood was set by the brilliant blue sky, the brash silver of the cannery sheds against the dusty green of the swamp woods, and by the elegance and smartness of the pineapple plants themselves, which extended in endless straight rows. The children had made pineapple cutouts of colored papers.

Between these rows sat the cauga remnants. On a plaid blanket were a freshly baked bread and piles of fruit. The wine was a fiery palm wine, not the familiar sendi.

Tattattatha's talk to the folk was "On Agriculture." As always the words were accompanied by his flute and by the musing of his "breath spaces," and so seemed to have only a rambling continuity. In the years to come, members of the households were to remember only certain parts of the homily, or to remember it differently.

TATTATTATHA'S SAYINGS

With this wine and this bread we offer ourselves. The baking oven and the wine press are not the work of our hands only.

•

We are sitting at a common table, even though we are not all of us here. If this is our last meal and we are leaving—then for those who are staying it is also the last meal.

•

The "cauga" is not real. It is only a symbol of the real. That is what makes it sacred.

•

In the candle's smoke the Ancestors became myth figures. But you are moving into myth, merely by stepping beyond this field.

•

These lovely dances are being performed by the animals for us. The hyena still laughs and steals. The hornbill is shrewd. The anteater resists. But the antelope no longer plows the soil with its hooves. How alienated we have become!

•

We live in a diminished totality. What we think now, and the system in which we think it, merely catalogues what remains. With the original paradise in fragments, what can we remember? And who do we become as we remember it?

•

Individuality is merely a stage in process of social breakdown.

•

Because man originally felt himself identical to the animals, his mind feeds on metaphor.

•

The amazing bird flies, the fish leaps, the reptile sheds his skin.

•

Without transcendence, the world of fact would choke us.

•

How shall I orient myself in the three regions? In the landscape where I go, under every bush, some god or spirit animal has left a footprint.

•

The Blue shaman weaves. The Yellow shaman unweaves.

•

The Blue shaman: growth, joy.
The Yellow shaman: compression, power.

•

The veil hides. The web knits together.

•

Society recycles itself through the age grades. Nature recycles itself through the swamp.

•

If there were a kingdom of Decay, its highways would be the great tides and its signposts the empty shells left by the migrants on the way.

•

The salmon leaps and spawns. The body is reclothed easily.

•

The process of recycling is the swamp. The reclothing and re-embodiment of souls is accomplished elsewhere.

•

Communards, you are not dying, you are only emigrating. Your guides will suffer the loss for you.

•

Be of good cheer. As you leave this place you are carrying the Ancestors with you. You are only looking for your bodies.

•

Two oceans were crossed over. The Atlantic was a Lethian stream in which we forgot Europe. The Pacific was a Lethian stream in which we forgot America. And now you are going back there, with your eyes opened.

•

Inside the mountain: the storehouse of souls. The Lake Outside and beyond the mountain: the tumbling River.

•

In the spinning cataract the ferryman goes through light years.

SWAMP INHABITANTS

They had been traveling in the swamp for some days. The bamboo continued. The enormously tall canes in clumps stood straight up overhead on patches of higher ground. These were called hammocks. Between these the flats were covered with saw grass. Here the ground was relatively hard and the grass matted with tracks. Runnels of watery mud extended up into the grass, and into these the swamp drained.

The bands voyaged mostly in shade. Was it the feathery gloom that affected vision, or had the atmosphere altered in some way? The overtopping bamboo shaded the flats with their deep, dark grass. Sometimes there was an opening. The grass lightened in color, and the runnels with their oily film of decaying vegetation gave off a rainbow hue.

The route skirted the hammocks and was built up with logs over wet spots. There were increasing stretches traversing the open. The tree-topped hammocks would recede, and appear in the distance like islands over the horizon of grass. The grass was waist high.

Then they plunged into the woods again. The bamboo which bordered the swamp had given way to hardwoods, live oaks, and mahogany. They were on higher ground. Perhaps these were islands in the swamp with their own climates. Or perhaps they were the end of some wandering peninsula, attached somewhere to the mainland of Nghsi-Altai.

• •

The sacred "cauga"—so constituted by Tattattatha—had been walking together in a band since the beginning of the swamp journey.

A troupe of monkeys raced overhead. "Why, listen to them scream! How nimble they are," remarked one of the women from the Fire phratry who had been walking beside Sathan and Maddi. "They're like birds."

Indeed the monkeys, swinging from branch to overhanging branch, seemed to spend as much time in the air as birds. And when they lighted, the branch was barely weighted down.

The woman's children, who were called Pulin and Mukh, had made friends with the Harditt children since the pilgrims had entered the swamp.

The monkeys had descended. It seemed the monkey band was now directing the caravan, leading the way down the road. A monkey family was walking with Lucia and Maddi. The rest of the households were laughing at their antics, which seemed to mimic the walkers. When they left, Maddi's purse was gone.

•   •

One of the new Sky clansmen was the first to notice the bear. The man had been making the journey that day with Venu and Rathlee Golla.

The column was at the edge of a wood and had been skirting a creek. The man pointed, and there in the middle of the creek was a bear, unconcernedly fishing. The big animal had a simple, somewhat droll expression on his face and looked almost human. They noted he had slyly chosen a shady spot in the creek so as not to show his reflection.

The cover had gotten denser, the trunks vine-covered and the ground wetter. It had been some time since the caravan had been in an open section of the swamp.

With only several of the bands visible, and with the track wandering aimlessly among the dim woods, the Sawna folk felt they had lost all sense of time.

In the middle of the path sat a lion. The lion did not move. He sat upright over his kill, the tail feather of a peacock sticking out the side of his mouth. The formal amber-colored mane made him look as if carved. The lion's eyes were closed.

The wall of the wood was steamy and stippled. Vines twisted around the trees. It was all leaves and stripes. Leopards moved liquidly against the camouflage, and creatures who seemed to be nothing more than some furtive and fleeting presence coalesced into eyes. These eyes of tigers burned like fires.

The column of pilgrims were standing with their feet in the water. They had been marching since early morning under a bank along the edge of a creek.

86

Pelicans rose squawking. They were apparently at the mouth of a larger creek or river. The reedy bank had been dug away, further up a waterfall sounded, though it could not be seen. Through a lip of grasses higher up there was a sheen of light on some wider open space.

In the foreground a pair of long-necked eland browsed among the leaves. The color of their hides was dark chocolate and tan, and their horns, though coming to a sharp point, were turned as on a lathe. On the sun-drenched plain behind them a herd of antelope grazed.

Then the animals were running away. They were slowly moving off into the distance in straight lines. With their heads down they seemed to be ploughing the savanna grass—or showing the art of plowing.

Were the animals real? Venu discussed the question with the newly substituted Sky man and with Rathlee Golla.

Rathlee was of the opinion that they were "spirit animals," brought here by the shamans for their inspection. Probably the shamans merely wished to display them to the exiles of Nghsi at this point in their journey. But they were undoubtedly there. In any case, the members of the caravan together had seen the animals.

But they had seen them as aesthetic objects. These animals on the tranquil plain were splendid, and those in the dreaming shade also seemed to have been placed there as in a painting.

What was perhaps most strange: everyone had recognized the animals. They were species which the plainsmen had never seen in real life. Nevertheless they had seen them accurately portrayed, in a characteristic pose or gesture, in the shaman dances. Some of them were clan "Ancestors." The animals had long since vanished from their familiar habitat, but were still remembered in the dances.

Now, with the appearance of the totem animals, the onlookers seemed to have been thrown back into another period of time. In fact, to the time of the Ancestors.

•   •

They had been traveling for a week through cypress and mangrove woods. The mangroves were raised; the roots were the perches of birds and small animal nests. The trunk of the trees sent out props, and the lower branches of the red mangrove reached down stilts into the mud. Thus the woods were actually lifted. They appeared to be suspended in air.

Late one day the column left behind the mangroves and struck out through swampy pools. It was after sundown, and they could actually see the sky through the trees' roots.

They were in a wide half-submerged bog with islands of grass on the far side. The sky was glowing. In the bog the "swamp lavender" flowers burned in the lurid light, and looking back it seemed that the black water under the trees was rising.

During the first days of exile, after the lottery losers had left Sawna, traveling through the other villages of the county they had had the illusion that the very soil was drifting away in the wind. And now in the twilight it seemed the mangrove forest had floated off.

After that everything was saw grass. The terrain through which the caravan passed was more level and also lower. It seemed as if now, with nothing but the grass, the landscape had become simplifed.

One of their shaman guides told them that having left the woods behind and having witnessed the ancestral animals, the band was entering the second stage of their swamp journey.

"From now on," he said, "you will begin to see objects as water."

• •

The drainage channels increased. After a while the caravan took to the channels. The only skyline was the feathery tips of the spartina grass. The bank also was held by the tough, deep-delving grass.

A moisture hung in the air, and seemed to wash up into the air. It seemed that the bank itself was no longer composed of solid earth. In the spaces between the soil grains there was water, and in the binding roots there was also water being pulled up through the stems and capillaries. Air and earth interfaced through the wet membrane. Water pressed to the top and evaporated into air, and

88

through the membranes below, the water of the swamp, slightly salty, was sucked in.

Even the structure of the Spartina was water-bound. The water coalesced into these shapes of stems and spiky blades. It was as if the travelers were seeing, like an aura, the watery shapes of the plants.

After traveling long days in this way under the banks, they began to develop eyes for small things. In the week before, passing beneath mangroves they had hardly noticed the roots crusted with coon oysters. Now they felt, through the smallest life, the processes of the swamp. At the cool base of the spartina, the melampus snail fed on the detritus made by the decayed grass. The snail would rest and hide from the sun at midday, then climb the stem of the plant in the afternoon, along with the periwinkle. A beetle foraged among the roots. Nearby a clam worm left a trail of mucus on the mud. Transparent lice sucked the plant stems. The kernels of the seed stalks were cracked by frit larvae; and above, swarms of small flies hung like wisps of smoke over the marsh.

In the water too there were the countless small creatures and larvae that fed the fish. Water boatmen and whirligigs. The mosquito wriggler hung head down, pulling particles into its mouth and breathing through its tail from a tube. Anemones withdrew into the mud. They began seeing the ghostly shrimp.

●　　●

The Harditt band had had a number of shaman guides since the plains region. A guide would accompany the column for a certain stage, then be replaced by another. There was no attempt to assign one guide permanently to a group of lottery losers.

During the nights the shaman guides preferred not to stay in the camp but returned to one of the swamp islands. Possibly there were shaman settlements on the islands, which were used as bases for rest and to resupply the pilots of the caravan as it advanced in stages through the swamp country toward the border.

One late afternoon some Sawna women went down to the creek. The camp was pitched not far from a decaying pier. Here they found the shamans "looking at microorganisms."

They were using their third eye, their own guide explained to Nanda, to extend the visual spectrum so they could see objects of only a few microns' width.

"What is the third eye?" another of the Fourth Grade women asked Nanda. Nanda, who had seen the shaman on the trip find the lost handkerchief, also with his third eye, was at a loss to explain.

"And what do the shapes look like?"

The shamans only smiled.

What the shamans were experiencing seemed to be mostly an aesthetic pleasure. Their eyes almost closed, they were lying on the docks face down, squinting between the boards.

The shamans left soon after for one of their swamp islands.

That night it was hot. The women were having trouble sleeping. Sathan got out from under her mosquito net. Nanda and Bhungi, her granddaughter, joined her. The child trailed around the grass in her bare feet, holding her nightgown up so that it would not get wet from the dew.

They decided to wake the Fire woman and Bhungi's friend, Pulin, and go down to the creek again for a swim before dawn.

They slipped out of their clothes and left them on the bank. Stepping into the pool, they felt the softness. Though the creek was deep at this point, still the women could touch bottom. Sathan slowly paddled as her sister held up Bhungi. The child lay on the water trailing her hair.

The world was quiet. Sathan pushed her arms forward, then pulled them gently back. As she did so, her body seemed to lighten. In the great stillness of the swamp, she seemed to be the only thing moving.

When they returned to the bank their mosquito lamps had gone out. It was lighter. In the air somewhere birds were chorusing.

The stars had faded. Imperceptibly the sky had lost its transparency and grown milky. Above their heads, the outline of the swamp grasses began to appear.

A hazy light hung over the swamp, and now they could begin to see their own bodies, yet these were part of the milky dawn light. At the same time the stalks and leaves of the spartina became palpable.

The three women and the two children sat on the bank watching and feeling the first warmth.

There was a quickening flush over the sky, then the first sun struck the tops of the spartina.

The sun's rays struck the bank, and as the sun rose, its rays moved further and further down into the pool.

"Look!" exclaimed the Fire woman. "Can you see them?"

There was a line. On one side the pool was darkly still. And on the other side there was an active kinetic zone. During the night the energy-giving sediments had filtered down the underwater slope. The photoplankton were becoming active.

Light struck the minute silica skeletons of the diatoms and turned the mud gold. Where the bathers had stepped and scraped the bottom, there were purple ribbons and splotches. It was the hue of the exposed sulphur photosynthetic bacteria. Heat quickened the organisms. Sheets of blue-green algae shone from within the saw grass litter.

Above stretched the leaves of the grass that would die down to litter. Through the leaves the flower stalks were thrust up. On their threadlike stems pollen chambers were open and trembling, loosing pollen grains into the air in an invisible cloud.

The women also seemed to be dissolving and loosening in the first light of morning.

• •

Even the saw grass had been left behind. The ground rose and fell, but it could not be called a landscape, alternating between sun-heated pools and higher muddy flats baked by the sun.

During the early stages of the journey the shaman Elwood had given a dog's spirit reading for a child. Because of his bad eyesight he could hardly see the child or the dog. Nevertheless he had seen their "auras." During the swamp journey the shaman's eyesight had declined further. Leading the exile column along the marsh

91

trails, their guides proceeded mostly "by feel." They seemed almost blind to their visual surroundings.

Were they then seeing the auras of the swamp, in particular the plants' and insects' auras? Were there to be other auras? Or were they using some other mode of perception?

One day the marchers were pursuing a muddy channel when Elwood, who had been leading the Ladpur "cauga," held up his hand. Before them stretched an alligator. She had laid her eggs and covered them in a heap of mud and decaying vegetable matter. This compost as it rotted produced heat, and the heat incubated the eggs.

The immobile female alligator, herself covered and caked with mud, seemed barely alive. Vapors of steam rose above the incubating mounds.

What the marchers noticed was that the shaman had not *seen* the animal. His eyes, caked with mud, were not even open. It was the heat that he had sensed, and that had caused him to stop and have them detour around the alligator.

Just as the Blue shamans were Weather and Soil sensors, were the Yellow shamans then heat sensors? Not oriented toward to track of the visible, nor following a compass direction, they seemed to be pursuing some other mode. Their response was to something felt through the pores and membranes like an osmotic pull, the lessening of a pressure gradient.

• •

The folk had continued their practice of telling their dreams and the myth stories. But the myths—whose origins were with the Blue shamans and which signified obscurely the Daily Lives in Nghsi-Altai—had become barely relevant. As to the Yellow shaman myth cycle, was it to be played out here in some manner?

They had now reached the "Kingdom of Decay," their shaman pilot had told them. The Sawna folk, who had come already through several stages, guessed that this must be one of the last stages of the exile voyage.

In past days the water in the marsh had grown brackish. But there were no tides. The salt, they conjectured, must be leached from the agricultural lands from which the wastes and sediments drained off, through the muddy channels into the swamp basin.

After the encounter with the alligator, their track lay along a section of swamp where on one side was bog or peaty muck. On the other side was a sheet of black water out of which rose a wood of dead trees. Hardly any branches remained, only the gray-green trunks were standing. On one of these a fisher hawk perched.

Beyond the flooded wood were more low flatlands covered with swamp lavender. And beyond that they could see open water, a stretch of pale steamy white that had no bounds or features and that seemed like the sea.

The shaman said: "All Nghsi drains into this. Toward the other side it is mostly salt. And there is the canal that leads to the cataract."

The day before the Yellow shaman had led them around the alligator, yet he was blind. The shamans were heat sensors. The band were in the place now where life decomposed, where all things burned with the slow combustion of decay.

"Wandering in the fields of hell, I came upon the realm Infrared"—one of Blake's songs had described.

The life processes burned—that is they passed energy on through the membranes activating one process after another. The sun and the atmosphere were one heat engine, but the internal processes of sentient and growing life were another. Here the energy gradient was always downward. Organized through the sun, as they burned the structures broke down through decay into their micro-elements, which were again recycled.

All of Altai, the biomes of the Plain, the Forest and Rift, drained into the swamp and were renewed.

The band had witnessed the shaman's knacker activities outside the villages, where they had burned the corpses. Now in the swamp, where everything was fluid and where plants and animals dissolved, they presided over the Decay Chains—just as the Blue shamans had presided over the growth chains, that is the building of structures and species.

In this way the exiles of Nghsi were being guided to the border, and perhaps were already experiencing what lay beyond the border.

MADDI'S CHILD

They were in open water, but the steamy mist had shut down around them. The liquid surface was light brown, streaked with yellow, and at intervals mottled with plants. Yet the channel or the several channels where they had been drifting must be deeper. Here the water was darker.

The landscape had vanished in steam—both the sky and the element on which they were being carried. Still, the "cauga" remnant on the raft seemed to have been brought closer.

The children floated gaily beside them. First Bhungi and Pulin, then Lal and Mukh, took turns riding on the back of a huge turtle.

Except for the sluggish underwater pull there was no movement. However, at intervals the steamy air would eddy and part. They could see they were passing between islands. Their banks rose distinctly from the swamp, but the places had no features. They were only mud. They were told that these were the islands of the Mud men.

Passing by one of these islands they were surprised to see naked figures. They were on the beach cooking. Near them were middens, piles of shells and bones where they had previously eaten, and what appeared to be a totem pole. The Mud men were making their supper in a huge pot from which steam rose, but there was no fire under it.

There were about twenty. Their bodies were completely encased in mud, and their genitals were covered by a branch also mud-smeared. It appeared that they were wearing masks and that these were made of the same light gray or whitish blue mud, stiffened into clay. But it was hard to tell because the faces were unformed and without features.

It was possible, too, that some of these figures were shamans. The islands, like the hammocks earlier, were the resting places of the guides during the steamy trip through the swamp. Perhaps they were their permanent abode. The mud islands were the place from which, perhaps, the Yellow shamans appearing at intervals in the country to escort the lottery losers had always come.

The steam was lifting. They were passing by other islands without figures, only the piles of shells to indicate that the Mud men had been there. There were the totem poles, as many as three or four on a single island. On one the Sawna folk passed so close that they could see the great wooden totem in detail. At the base was a terrapin or broad land turtle. On the back of that was a mullet with a wide-open mouth. On top of these two were a crab and then a beetle. Then there were carved shapes which were not recognizable, but which might have represented May fly larvae or bacteria of some kind.

The topmost figure was a kite.

It was appropriate that the Mud men, who were residents of the swamp and who presided over the cycles of decay, should erect such a symbol.

Some of the carvings were of the Mud men themselves. And some of them seemed to be of the shamans.

•   •

They had come to a place that was called Last Island. There the shamans made Maddi a hut under one of the totem poles. Her labor began on the next day.

The hut was constructed of reeds. Reeds and straw were spread on the floor.

Sathan and her aunt Nanda encouraged her. Maddi gritted her teeth and concentrated. Between the contractions she sipped juice and enjoyed the company gathered around her. Maddi, with her knees bent and her back resting against a board, was very much the center of attention.

A family of white-footed mice were already making use of the shelter. Perhaps they had been living on this same spot before. They seemed almost tame. A mouse scampered along the pole, stopped, and twitched its ears at Maddi.

Her stomach was enormously stretched. Ramdas kept rubbing powder on the taut skin. She felt her hair lank and damp but did not lift her hand to smooth it.

Maddi lay panting with her mouth open. When the pains came she moved her head from side to side. Ramdas thought her eyes were large. The envelope had broken, and the blanket under her legs was wet.

Her father, Venu, was bending over to give her juice, and for a moment she had him confused with her great-grandfather, Gopal Harditt. And Ramdas she mixed up with Reddi. The light was behind their heads, and it seemed to be coming through them.

Maddi smiled at the animals. The rest of the animals of the place had come, summoned no doubt by the mouse. As Maddi lay they looked at her. There was a muskrat and a racoon sitting on its haunches. Two muddy gray birds stared solemnly down at Maddi. One of them kept twisting his neck to peck at fleas.

Finally the contractions sharpened. Her stomach, as the muscles tensed and the pressure mounted against the cervix, was hard as a stone. Her fist was clenched around Sathan's. During the last stage she could feel the creature adjusting its head, and there was a deep sexual feeling in her vagina as the baby was pushed forward.

• •

Maddi woke with the baby cradled on her arm. The morning light stole through the cracks in the reed mat, stippling Maddi's breast and the baby.

During the evening before the Ancestors had come. She remembered seeing Reddi, one of the "last gones," and the old councilor. They also had been present with the animals.

And so this was Last Island. The hut was located on the shore, and the animals had come out of their holes and perches where they had been living. These were not the legendary beasts that the caravan had glimpsed when first entering the swamp, but the actual animals of the place—the residents. The thought made Maddi want to cry.

Yes. This is the last *place*. After this it will not be a place at all. It will be something different.

The Ancestors had come through the swamp to attend the childbirth. They had come from the Kansu region and had returned. As the pollen grains of the swamp grasses, lifted in the air, floated back over the plains, so the Ancestors had floated back. Like the pollen grains the members of the cauga band too had been loosened from their earthly soil and were now being dispersed toward America.

The visit of the Ancestors had been strengthening. She felt the strength, the pull of the line going back through time. The great-grandfather had been here, leaning beside the bed with his thin fingers and the veins bunched over the knuckles. He had reached down and smoothed Maddi's hair.

But for the Harditt toc, was this not also the last island? They could accompany the exiles only so far, and now they had reached the border. Were not they too "tied to earth?"

●　　●

The next day the "cauga" celebrated Kanagat. Also the Harditts had their child-naming.

During the swamp passage all the baggage had been relinquished except for the fragile family shrines made of bamboo and rice paper. After the last "ghost meal" even these were to be left behind. The cameos would dim, the burned joss sticks grow damp, and the colored streamers rot and unravel in the wind on the island shingle.

The new baby was called Gopal Harditt.

THE CITY OF BAKBAKWALANUSIWA

Already the waters surrounding Last Island were salt. The salt increased. Over the wide marsh, which extended back to the mainland, the bottom of the reeds and cattails were crusted with salt. As they reached to shore over the flats even the flowers were saltcaked.

The many "caugas" of lottery losers of the plains abandoned their rafts as they reached the shallows. Struggling toward the shore through the stiff reeds, there was a moment when the entire caravan seemed to disappear and become lost from each other.

The shore and the hills rising from the shore were a coarse naked sand.

Bunghi and Lal found themselves running up a line of dunes. There was in fact a wave of children running along the entire length of the beach, clambering up the dunes, calling and shouting to each other, and using their arms and legs in the loose sand. It was as if they had escaped and were impelled up after the long confinement on the rafts.

The two Harditt children had started out with Mukh and Pulin of the Fire woman's clan but had left them behind in the mad scramble up the beach. The sand grew looser and the flank of the dune steeper. The adults, far below on the shore, were coming ahead, but very slowly, as if unable to move out of the salt landscape.

They had reached the top. Here the dunes flattened to form a dyke. From the top of this, looking backward to the north over the wide basin of reeds, they could just see, barely visible on the horizon, the faint line of the mud islands.

On the opposite side was desert. The desert was flat sand at a level far lower than the inland sea. It was a grayish wan color and trackless, extending as far as the eye could see. Running straight along the bottom of the dyke was a canal, sunk in the stained sand.

The plane of the desert rose imperceptibly to the west. Here the surface was modeled into shifting hills.

Then they saw in the distance, struggling over the sand in a wavering line like ants, another of the exile caravans. And along the road, a third caravan of exiles was advancing.

The canal which lay along the bottom of the dyke was a continuation of the Nghsi River. The river passed through the Rift valley draining the Karst cities. The lakes and cantonments of the wilderness region were also drained by a tributary of the river which, circling in a wide arc, traced the western margin of the Drune. Then the wall of the forest ended and the land dwindled, first to low hills and then became dry scraggly mesa. At the point where the branches of the river joined, the desert began.

The wayfarers who had passed through the swamp struck out toward the east along the top of the dyke, above the others. For some days the march of the caravans from the Rift and the Drune was parallel.

Swarming up the dunes, the children had left behind Mukh and Pulin. And during the march along the dyke, the Harditts had become separated from several of the other clans which had composed the swamp-traveling "cauga."

Looking down one morning, the Sawna folk saw that the other two exile columns had joined. The next day all three caravans came together at a place where the dunes ended.

First the Sawna pilgrims had seen the shamans' skins stippled in the bamboo woods. Then they had become dirty and disfigured with brown streaks, passing through the mud islands, and had been blinded. And finally, on the water stretch of the journey, over the Sea of Reeds, the shamans' skin had become salt caked.

The long trek through the swamp had been as arduous for the shamans as for the pilgrims. And perhaps it was the shamans who were suffering the process of breakdown and recycling through the swamp. And now they were at the city which marked the end of the swamp journey.

The "cauga" remnant stood looking down at a lagoon. And on the other side of the lagoon was a city, constructed of reeds and cemented shells, but many of the buildings were vast. They appeared to be mostly warehouses. Behind the warehouses was a power station.

There were no compounds or point houses, as there were in the Rift cities of Altai. In front of the windowless warehouses stretched a long quay.

An array of boats ran out from the quayside. They were flat scows or sampans. The first rank was tied to the dock at the prow, and the rest extended back, lashed together side by side along the gunwales. The packed mass of boats extended out into the middle of the lagoon, cluttering it like a floating mat of lillies.

It was a city without inhabitants, an empty city. The Sawna families had been told it was a transhipment depot for souls. Was it, Motteram and Rathlee Golla wondered, a transhipment depot for the shamans as well?

• •

The caravan people had been gathered into the boats. Nanda and Rathlee's family were seated by the gunwale of one of the scows, crowded in with other families. It seemed to Nanda they were completely disoriented.

There was no order. Everyone had started clambering onto the boats at once. Nanda and Rathlee, together with Lucia and her family, stepped gingerly from the deck of one tipping sampan to the next. In the confusion they had almost lost Bunghi. The little girl, who had been clinging to her grandmother's hand, became separated from them only for a moment. They retrieved her, bawling. Motteram was carrying Lal on his shoulders.

These scows had flat open decks which rose slightly toward the bow and stern. They were sturdy and very battered and had evidently made the trip through the cataract many times. Along the gunwale, the deck was worn in a narrow track where the oarsmen or pilots had propelled the vessel with their long poles.

Night had settled over the lagoon. On top of the mast of Nanda's and Rathlee's boat was a lighted oil lantern. As the minutes passed, more lanterns were lighted.

Nanda Harditt, looking around the crowd, could see no sign of her sister's family.

101

There were no shamans within the boats. However, they had been at the quayside that afternoon. It had been at the command of the guides that the crowd of wayfarers had filled the boats.

The wide space in front of the warehouses was empty, and it appeared that the buildings were empty. Suddenly the quayside lighted up.

From the inside of the warehouses, from the roofs and basements, even—it seemed—from under their own boats, voices began to call. It was the high nasal calls of the Yellow shaman storytellers, their voices eerily projected.

The last one of the "earth leave-taking" or "capturing" dances of the Yellow Shaman Society was about to take place. Bunghi's arms tightened around her grandmother's neck. And Lal, clutching Motteram, began to whimper.

Though the unfamiliar setting heightened the drama's effect, the dances were the same ones that the Sawna folk had seen performed many times outside the villages of Kansu by the traveling troupes. A horde of terrifying and ferociously howling animals and birds erupted from the warehouses into the square. Among these was the cannibal bird, Bakbakwalanusiwa. But it was not one hapless villager being pounced on and eaten. In this case it was the shaman guides themselves. The entire length of the quay, before each section of the floating audience, performances were going on at once. Deafened by shrieks and assaulted by claws and beating wings and the tearing of beaks, the hapless victims were "captured." The former guides, surrounded by the Spirit Beings, were dragged bound into the boats.

Were these boats then destined for the "Under world"? Had the shaman guides, having been eaten by the cannibal bird Bakbakwalanusiwa and the other Spirit Beings, now acquired their potency and magical power to guide the boats during the descent through the cataract?

They were only ceremonial, these "earth leave-taking" dances. Yet there was no doubt that the travelers had gone through another step which approached the underground. And soon they would be traversing the world of spirits.

THROUGH THE CATARACT

The next day the flotilla left behind the empty city and proceeded through a series of locks to the canal, with the Spirit Beings "piloting" the boats. In their extravagant masks and regalia of feathers and skins, the Ancestral beings stood by the bows. Other shamans, now unshackled, manned the oars and sweeps.

Now at the level of the canal, they were at the back side of, and below, the city where the capturing dances had taken place. Looking up, the pilgrims could see an immense hydroelectric power station.

At a point below this was the outfall where the water, after passing from the lagoons to turn the turbines of the plant, gushed out in a torrent into the canal.

Standing high at the bow of each boat, with claws for hands and the visages of bears and hawks, their new pilots presented a fearsome sight. For the first time, the impending trip seemed terrifying.

"They have been eaten themselves. And now they are the eating ones," Rathlee Golla remarked to Motteram. It was clear that he felt himself victimized.

However, beyond the power outfall the flotilla halted. After guiding the boats for a short stretch, the old pilots disembarked and were replaced by new ones.

The journey toward the border continued.

• •

The water route had been wandering. Now they could see only a dozen or so of the other boats. The convoy had been separated. Though the river current moved rather slowly, many of the boats had evidently been carried on ahead.

The power outfall was behind. After the stage where they had let the pilots off, the deck of the river boat seemed even more crowded. The second branch of the Harditts sat close together. The Sawna folk were no longer with their plains clansmen. There were ten families on the deck. Several were Rift and Wilderness families.

Venu and Ramdas, their backs against some grain sacks, were discussing with Sathan the meaning of the capturing ceremony. Most of it was clear. They were forced to emigrate. Was it not an advantage, or at least a consolation, to have this event ratified by the power-giving birds?

Sathan said wryly, but with some puzzlement: "Yes. We are being exiled, and they are showing the way for us. But they are also forcing us."

Sathan thought that these guides were not like the others. They must be some kind of specialized shamans.

The faces of the new shaman pilots were those of young men and were quite plain. They had no special markings. They had come aboard with long poles, but these were not now in use. They had also carried some rotting grain sacks on board. A third pilot sat in the stern, guiding the boat with a long sweep.

The sturdy bamboo poles which were now lying on the deck were each about twenty feet long and capped with a steel tip.

The stream meandering between its banks flowed evenly. What had before been only a stagnant canal had now—with the added volume from the hydroelectrical plant outfall—become a sizable river.

Gradually the sound of the tumbling water spewing from under the plant receded, and its place was taken by another distant roaring, that of the Falls. Beyond the last city, the great basin of reeds also came to an end. This was the last border and the terminus of the inland sea as well. Here, over a basalt ledge and combed by cypress roots, the water concentrated at the lip of the hanging plateau of Altai and plunged over the Falls.

As the sound of the outfall diminished, that of the Falls, high overhead and to the left, kept getting louder.

Venu asked Sathan if she were thirsty. One of the Karst families had managed to bring a container of water on board and a Coleman stove. Otherwise, there were no belongings of the wayfarers on the river boat.

The river in a wide sweep was taking them in a direction away from the border. They were passing between banks of overhanging trees through which some farmland could be glimpsed. One of the pilgrims took out a harmonica.

The rough spritely tune and the glimpse of the plowed fields through the willows made Venu think of home. Instinctively he looked around for Motteram and the other Harditt family. But they were not to be located in the boat convoy.

The river wandered in great sweeps and sometimes deepened. And sometimes they rode over shallows where the pace quickened and the guides worked the poles. Then the placid drifting resumed.

The empty city and the power plant were behind. The squadron, taken along by a current which was sometimes barely perceptible, had nevertheless descended a good distance. They were now far below the level at which they had set out early that morning from the lagoons connecting to the Sea of Reeds.

The river had swung back toward the border. To their left and right the low hills which they had been passing through steepened abruptly.

The hillside had now become a ravine. Above were misty crags. Venu stared up at terraces built into the slope where there were tiny figures, and which he took to be corn or tobacco plots perhaps. Then it was only crags and trees. A high-tension line marched by over the firs. There was no further sign of life.

The gorge widened and straightened, and for an interval they could see ahead. The wall of mountains they had been approaching was now directly in front of them. The face was scarred as if by stone quarries and partly obscured, by mist. The river had widened and grown faster. It seemed that the river was entering the mountain through an enormous hole.

• •

There had been a strong current earlier, but now the gliding waters were almost smooth. The flotilla was reassembled again and could be made out by a long line of lights.

They were in a cavern. From the entrace through which they had come, light still diffused over the immense milky roof. Ramdas looking back could make out the outlines of the vast roof. Ahead there was only darkness. And the line of the lights and masts growing progressively smaller and dimmer.

• •

They were still under the mountain. Their own boat was in a roofed-over channel sliding between walls of black rock. Again they could hear the stunning roar of the falls above somewhere. The two shamans at the sides had moved apart. Every once in a while they would lean out and exert pressure against the rock with their poles. The shaman at the back had taken in his sweep and was also using his pole to fend off the boat from the wet walls.

The pull of the sluiceway was steady below them, it seemed as if they were racing. The other families, perhaps because they were crouching on the deck, could barely be seen. Ramdas could see Maddi, who was holding the small Gopal tight to her breast. Her back was wedged against Ramdas's leg.

Passing under these low places, where the limestone buttresses of the cavern stood close, the light on the mast of their small boat grew sharper and yellower. Ramdas could almost reach out and touch the wet face of the rock as it moved by.

• •

The squadron had taken a turning. Here there were no openings to the light and no current. There seemed to be no will to move in the stillness of this underground lake or series of lakes. It seemed not to be a place they had come to or would ever leave.

The clear air was laden with cold.

Ramdas watched the shamans, who were sitting idly. Wavering patterns and oscillations of light came from the water itself and played against the roof of the cavern and against the ship's sides.

The shamans had stopped poling and were sitting along the gunwale with their feet in the water. Moving their feet playfully, they stirred streams of luminescence. Their poles which now lay on the deck seemed also to be a source of illumination.

He stood watching the play of light-shapes over the vast roof. There seemed to be an infinity of shapes.

"We are in the storehouse of souls."

Ramdas also remembered the phrase, "shapes are changed."

The play of light appeared to come from the surface only of the underground lake. Below it was cold and dark. No doubt, on the floor of the cavern also the illuminations played.

A coldness gripped him. Though there were other figures on the deck, he seemed to be the only one living. In any case, he was alone.

Was it on this lake that the dead were recycled after being dissolved in the chemistry of the swamp? It was possible that, for all the others of the land of Altai who had come this way through the timeless cave, piloted by the shamans, it had been to undergo death and re-creation.

The lake and perhaps the mountain were beyond time. But they were moving out of it. Still living, they were passing *through* Under world. But to where?

He remembered what Tattattatha had said: "Remember, in the new place you carry your souls with you. You are only looking for your bodies."

•   •

The last sluiceway was behind them. The rock walls had rushed apart. The sampan, plunging and sliding, rode on an expanse of foam. They were riding down the center of the cataract at tremendous speed.

The boat was in a kind of trough, as if there were a river within a river—depressed and constrained at the lower level by the element of sheer speed, by its rushing load. Washing back against the shore, there was another river which seemed to be held there in suspension, or even moving backward.

Beneath them the boat plunged and slid. It veered among mounds of water which excploded over the rocks. The current boiled around the Yellow shaman's poles as the shamans themselves leaned out over it tilting and lunging.

In the hands of the plunging shamans, the poles seemed to lengthen and grow taller. The figures, moving at such speed, seemed to be pure concentrations of force. And the cataract itself like some spinning black hole.

Then quickly it became lighter. The two rivers had subsided into one again. The walls at the sides became clearly visible. Then they were out and into the sunlight.

•   •

They were through and in the sunlight.

High overhead the mist drifted from the lip of the Falls over the forest. It was a white silky mist, but even so it partly obscured the high falls. The sound of the falls was partly muted.

The river, white and glassy, flowed between banks below which the green of the forest was reflected. The obscure forest green was also partly clouded as the mist at the bottom of the Falls boiled up and settled back.

Evidently some fish had leaped into the boat as they had passed the cataract. On the deck one of the Karst families was collecting them and putting them in a pail.

On the deck still lay the grain sacks. Evidently these were meant for them to exchange in the coastal cities, for their passage perhaps.

The shamans' poles were gone. However, the sweep was lashed to the stern where the shaman had left it. One of the passengers took this up and began to move the river boat through the gorges.

END OF BOOK IV

Exile is the fourth book of the tetralogy DAILY LIVES IN NGHSI-ALTAI.

The books were published, respectively, in 1977, 1978, and 1979 by New Directions.

Red Shift: An Introduction to Nghsi-Altai (1977) has been published by Penny Each Press, Thetford, Vermont 05074.

Complete descriptive catalog available free on request from
New Directions, 80 Eighth Avenue, New York 10011

† **Bilingual**